"If you knew me on a more...intimate basis, we might..."

"Go to bed?" Nora said with reckless bravery.

"That would be nice." He chuckled.

She refused to look into his warm eyes, so deep and dark that she might drown in them. She bent down to pick up her shoes, and Alec was beside her in an instant, catching her hand and holding it tight as a clap of thunder reverberated through the house.

"Leave them there. I like you better with them off. With everything off..."

Joan Lancaster is an animal lover who lives with her husband and daughters on a farm in rural Georgia. An avid fancier and breeder of purebred dogs, Joan has bred over one hundred champions of record and written several books on dogs. She travels as often as possible, and works full time for a major air-line.

Dear Reader:

Signs of spring are popping up all over—what a relief!—and this month's six SECOND CHANCE AT LOVE romances are brimming with all the elements that make radiant love stories. So choose a sunny corner, make yourself comfortable, and enjoy...

We begin with *Ain't Misbehaving* (#256), another heartwarming read from Jeanne Grant. All-man Mitch Cochran is captivated by gregarious Kay Sanders, but he has a problem. A long-term illness, from which he's fully recovered, kept him bedridden during the years when other young males were struttin' their stuff. Now he's somewhat chagrined to find himself a virgin at 28! To our delight, Jeanne Grant tackles this sensitive subject with tenderness, humor, and masterful skill.

Our next romance, *Promise Me Rainbows* (#257), is by Joan Lancaster, a new writer whose wacky, wonderful story is filled with lovable, eccentric characters. A runaway chimp, two giant St. Bernards, and a mysterious "fairy godmother" keep the action lively, while Alec Knowles's hot-blooded pursuit of feisty Nora Flynn ensures that the romance is offbeat and steamy.

In *Rites of Passion* (#258) by Jacqueline Topaz, Corky Corcoran's life of barely controlled suburban chaos becomes even crazier when she falls head over heels for brilliant, sexy anthropologist Kristoffer Schmidt. This romance has one of the funniest scenes of madcap domestic catastrophe I've ever read. Don't worry, I won't give the surprise away, but I will promise that once you've read *Rites of Passion* you'll never again think of anthropology as a dry-as-dust science!

In *One in a Million* (#259) by Lee Williams, heroine Suzannah isn't rich, but she's having a ball playing the part of a wealthy socialite on her aunt's estate—until her Rolls Royce breaks down in Craig Jordan's humble back yard. Suzannah hires Craig as a gardener and has fun playing a grand lady to his deferential servant. But soon deception piles on deception, and Suzannah becomes determined to exact revenge—with hilariously calamitous results!

In *Heart of Gold* (#260), Liz Grady once again creates a hero you can't help falling in love with. Roarke Hastings, handsome and self-assured, enrolls in Tess Maxwell's dance school to tame his two left feet ... and learns she's a damsel in distress. But are his offers of knightly assistance an expression of true love, or only of heart-felt kindness? Be assured, Liz Grady has written one powerful romance!

Finally, in *At Long Last Love* (#261) Carole Buck presents a funny, moving story of a friendship that blossoms into love. Allie Douglas and her boss, Chris Cooper, have been buddies for years, but something strange is happening to their comfortable companionship. Will it destroy their camaraderie or lead to a more exciting union? Carole Buck's realistic yet thoroughly entertaining approach to her subject makes *At Long Last Love* a special treat.

So, please do get outside and enjoy the fine weather, but don't miss any of this month's SECOND CHANCE AT LOVE romances. And thanks to all of you for sending the hundreds of questionnaires and letters we continue to receive. We love hearing from you!

Warm wishes,

Ellen Edwards

Ellen Edwards, Senior Editor
SECOND CHANCE AT LOVE
The Berkley Publishing Group
200 Madison Avenue
New York, N.Y. 10016

Second Chance at Love®

PROMISE ME RAINBOWS

JOAN LANCASTER

A SECOND CHANCE AT LOVE BOOK

Chapter 1

IT WAS RAINING cats and dogs by the time Nora's old van turned onto Peachtree Street. Which way was Symphony Hall anyway? She'd been there once a long time ago, before she'd split up with Doug and left New York. Before her parents had died and she'd moved back to their farm. Now everything was different. Atlanta wasn't the way she remembered it and she was living alone in the boondocks of Georgia. If you could call sharing your life with animals living alone. *Animals!* The reason she'd driven sixty miles on a stormy night. Thunder cracked, and the traffic slowed to a standstill in the teeming rain. The concert would be starting soon, and her friend Eve would be worried. Just her luck. Stuck in a Friday night traffic jam in downtown Atlanta and almost out of gas.

Lightning flashed and thunder boomed; the van's wipers squealed as they worked at full speed. She hated storms. Feared them. Especially the electrical kind. She tensed up and leaned forward on the wheel, unable to see clearly because of the rain coming down. The car in front of her seemed to be stalled.

"Move!" she said impatiently, perturbed by the shiny white foreign car that refused to budge, while her ten-year-old van groaned dependably. A hand jutted out of the window of the white car, and a tall man wearing a raincoat jumped out and came running toward her in the rain, dark haired and hatless, his head down.

"Could you give me a push, mister?" he asked. He looked at her through her window, his face screwed up with worry. "My motor's flooded."

Mister! "Yes." She nodded, annoyed because he'd mistaken her for a man, but unable to say so because her window was broken and wouldn't roll down.

"Thanks!" he yelled, flipping the collar of his coat up and pressing a big hand to her window. She looked at herself in the mirror, and realized she was still wearing her father's old rain hat, the one she wore when she had to run to the barn in a downpour. Her foot relaxed on the brake and she let the van roll forward. She tilted her face toward the beam of her headlights. Her wide-set green eyes sparked with fire; they were keenly alive and intelligent. Irish eyes. To go with her temper. Her lips tightened, and she turned her head from side to side. She'd stuffed her long chestnut hair under the hat to keep it dry, but she didn't *look* like a man. Did she?

"Hey! Take it easy!" the man in the white car yelled as her van bumped his car with a thud. Stomping her foot on the brake, she stared back at him. What did he want from her, wrecker service? He was coming toward her again and she glanced at the fuel gauge. Two more cups of gas and *she'd* be the one asking for a push.

"Could you try not to do that again, mister?" He squinted his eyes, and his brows came together as he studied her through the window. He held his face close to the glass in an attempt to see her more clearly. His bushy brows ruffled. "Your bumper's not hitting mine just right. If you're not careful you're going to smash in my lights!"

"Do you want a push or don't you?" she shouted through the narrow crack at the top of her window. She pulled off the yellow rain hat and allowed her long, naturally curly hair to fall over her shoulders. "I'm about out of gas myself."

"Excuse me, *miss*," he said apologetically, squinting harder to get a better look. "It's kind of hard to see out here in this rain. I wonder if you could push me into that station up ahead?"

She glanced at the GULF sign through the gray rain and back at him. "Okay, okay, just get going, will you?"

"Thanks!" he yelled, pressing his hand to her window again and running back to his car. She rolled the van forward carefully. "Your bumper's not hitting mine just right," she mimicked in his deep voice, looking in the mirror. What nerve! He was lucky she was nice enough to help him on a night like this. She prayed the last half-cup of gas would last until she reached the station, and sighed with relief when they began moving, her van pushing his car into the station as he waved from his window. "You're welcome!" she muttered, glad to be rid of him. Only then did she notice that his car had an out-of-state plate.

She reached for her purse and slipped her hand inside its cool interior, her face registering shock. No wallet, no money, no change! Nothing but the ticket Eve had given her for the concert and the letter from Doug Dunning, together with the facts and figures for the animal shelter she wanted to build. She'd forgotten everything else in her mad scramble to get out of the house on time.

"Fill it up, lady?" The gas station attendant was holding a hose in his hand. She managed to roll her window down an inch, which brought rain pouring in on her five-year-old suit, wetting her thoroughly. "You're not going to believe this, sir, but I forgot my—"

"Fill it up for her!" shouted the man in the white car, standing in the rain talking to a mechanic who bent to look under the car's hood. She gave the stranger an embarrassed smile and waved her hand in a gesture of gratitude, looking down at her watch without seeing the time. She certainly hadn't expected him to *fill* her tank. A couple of gallons would have been enough to get her to Symphony Hall, where her friend, Eve, would have given her some money.

"Could I ask another favor of you, miss?" *He was back!* She looked up to see him squinting at her through the window with a deep furrow between his brows, "Would you roll your window down so we could talk?"

"It's broken," she said, eyeing him suspiciously. "I can hear you just fine."

"The mechanic says my car will be here till tomorrow, and it would take a taxi more than an hour to get here in this rain. If you'd drop me off at Symphony Hall, I'd be most grateful. I'd pay you, of course." He reached inside his coat.

Symphony Hall was where *she* was going, but she didn't want him to know that. She'd learned some bitter lessons about men—especially from her ex-boyfriend, Doug, who'd gotten rid of her cat and wouldn't tell her what he'd done with it. Good old faithful Doug, who she'd caught in bed with a lady lawyer. Dear, sweet, generous Doug, who'd insisted on loaning her the money she'd needed to pay off the mortgage on her parents' farm and now demanded it back with interest. Her sense of betrayal was compounded because she'd loved him.

"I'm sorry, I can't," she said.

"Please." He gave her a grin that made her weak. "I'll give you fifty dollars."

Nora thought what she could do with fifty dollars. Buy dog feed, cat feed, hay for the horses. It had been a rough winter, and she'd borrowed steadily from Eve. She was feeding over a hundred mouths a day, sixty-four dogs, four horses, thirty-two cats, and two rabbits; unless Mr. and Mrs. Bunny had had their babies by now. And that didn't count the flying squirrel she'd crawled up in the attic to save one freezing night. But she'd promised herself never to trust a man again.

"I don't pick up strangers," she said, forcing herself not to look at him.

"But I'm not a stranger." He grinned. "At least I don't feel like one. Look, here's my I.D. I'm in town on business with the Center for Disease Control. I'm a doctor. I work for them." He held up his driver's license, and she took a good look. He appeared safe enough, standing there in the pouring rain with dimples in his cheeks and water running down his nose. An affable hunk who would have made most women throw open their doors and drag him inside.

"If you work for the CDC, why do you have Pennsylvania plates?"

"Pennsylvania's my permanent address. I'm in town for reassignment." He frowned at her. "My name's Alec Knowles." He shook the rainwater from his wallet and raised one brow. "You must be Nora."

She regretted the day she'd painted NORA'S ARK on the side of her van with the awful picture of a raft overflowing with dogs and cats. She'd done it herself to save money. She'd hoped the sign would alert people to what she was doing. Yes, she was Nora. The crazy lady from Walton County who collected strays, anything with sad eyes that needed a home. "That's me," she admitted. "And I'd like to help, really I would. But you could have found that wallet anywhere."

"I'm who I say I am, honest. I've been with the CDC for ten years. Since I got out of med school actually." He grinned, and her hands tightened on the wheel. "I'm just a Northerner in a southern town on his way to hear some good music." His face lit up as if he'd suddenly remembered something; reaching inside his raincoat, he pulled out a ticket—white, like the one Eve had given Nora for the concert. "Here! This proves I'm telling the truth. It's for tonight's performance at Symphony Hall."

"That'll be forty-seven twenty-two, mister," the attendant said, holding out his hand in the rain. "The lady's got a big tank."

"I didn't need all that," Nora protested.

"Forget it; it's the least I can do." Alec Knowles paid the attendant and put his wallet away, stuffing his hands in his raincoat pockets and turning to leave.

"They had a tornado on the other side of town," the attendant said. "You'd best be careful, young lady. It's a bad night to be out alone."

"I guess I could drop you off since it's so close," Nora told Alec, dropping her hand to the floor and snapping her fingers. A big dog in the back of the van sat up and opened his eyes. "I'm so late now it won't make much difference."

"Thanks!" His smile was dazzling as he ran around the van to the passenger side. Nora reached across the seat to lift the latch, and the huge, shaggy dog stood up and stretched.

"Wolf won't bite unless I scream," Nora warned. She snapped her fingers, and the massive tawny dog jumped over to the front seat and stood up with his front paws on the back of the seat beside her. "He's trained for attack in case you're thinking of trying anything."

"Don't worry," Alec said, stepping into the van and sitting very still as the dog hung its wedgelike head over his shoulder and smelled his hair. "What kind of dog is he?"

"A French briard, rare around here. But better protection than a gun. They're bred to kill wolves." She gave him a dirty look and started the motor. The van rattled and shot forward before Alec could get the door closed.

"Interesting," he said, holding onto his seat and the door handle as the van roared down the rain-slicked street. Wolf was licking his face as the van jerked abruptly to a stop. Nora glanced from the red light to Alec, who was still trying to close the door, the huge dog's paws draped around his neck. She struggled to keep from laughing. "Does it always rain this hard in Georgia?" he asked.

"It's spring," she answered, trying to concentrate on

the light. "Tornado season. This is only a frog strangler."

He laughed, and the light turned green. The van jumped forward as his dark eyes roamed over her, taking in her flat-heeled shoes and long stockinged legs, moving upward slowly to her knees, her thighs, and the big yellow raincoat with the collar that almost hid her face.

"I'm sorry I mistook you for a man back there. With all this rain and that hat pulled down over your hair, I couldn't see."

"Symphony Hall," she announced, surprised that it had been just down the street all along. She pulled over to the curb to let him out, and Wolf slid sideways, hanging onto Alec's neck for support.

"I insist you take this for your inconvenience." Alec reached into his pocket and pulled out a fifty dollar bill, leaning forward and laying it on the dash, Wolf still hanging on.

"It's my good deed for the day." She gave him back the money she needed so badly and smiled, their hands touching lightly. "I never charge for helping the weaker sex." She saw curiosity gleaming in his eyes, and admired the way they crinkled at the corners. He was so handsome he took her breath away. His straight black hair glistening in the street lights was wet with rain. It flicked down over his forehead in a way that accentuated his attractiveness. Wolf licked the side of his face with his big tongue. Alec tried to push the dog away, but Wolf kept licking.

"I have this thing about paying for services rendered." He gave her a look that reminded her she was a woman. "I don't usually leave a lady alone when there's a tornado brewing. Come inside, won't you? We'll see about getting you a seat, and we can go out for dinner and a drink afterward."

"Thanks, but I have other plans." She snapped her fingers, and Wolf jumped down and barked, wagging his tail.

"I think Wolf wants me to stay." Alec grinned, and she thought she would slide off her seat. "Maybe you'd like some time to think about it.''

"Good-bye, Doctor Bowles," she said, gunning the motor. Alec opened the door and stepped into the street.

"Knowles!" he called, but she drove off just as he closed the door.

"Men!" Nora sighed, taking a last look in the mirror at probably the handsomest man she'd ever see. Alec was standing in the street waving his arms in the air, yelling something she couldn't understand. Wolf licked her hand and jumped up into the vacated seat beside her, observing her with possessive eyes. "You're all alike," she told the dog, reaching over to pat Wolf's muzzle. "Every last one of you."

The FULL sign at the entrance to the parking lot made Nora angrier. She'd been stupid to pick up a man she didn't know. The Bowles guy could've been a murderer or worse. Dear God, she was dumb! Didn't she know criminals could be good looking and charming? The hunk's face filled her mind, and she tossed her dad's rain hat on the floor, noticing a white ticket on the mat beside it. Her ticket? No, *his* ticket! He'd left it behind in her van, and now she'd have to return it. Damn!

She found a parking place three blocks down the street and ran through the pouring rain to the hall. She was nearly an hour late. Eve would think she'd been in an accident. The rain was cold, and she was soaked to the skin by the time she reached the main door. She'd surely missed the beginning of the concerto, but thank goodness she could still meet the rich woman Eve had told her about, the one she was counting on to save her farm and build the animal shelter.

The lobby was empty when she stepped inside the glass doors and took off her coat. Sloshing across the thick red carpet to the ladies' room, Nora saw a man standing in a phone booth with the door open, his tan raincoat and slick black hair still wet with rain.

"I didn't know it was raining so hard," a little old lady commented as Nora pushed through the door marked LADIES and hurried to the mirror.

"I couldn't find a parking space," Nora replied, pulling her wet hair off her neck and surveying the damage. Her hair hung like a horse's tail over her chest, and her skirt was clinging to her legs.

"Don't worry, dear," the little old lady said sweetly. "The guest soloist was held up by the weather too. You haven't missed a note."

"I haven't?" Nora's face brightened.

"No, dear." The little old lady smiled and watched Nora smooth out her wrinkled stockings and tap the face of her drenched watch. "Atlanta's not the only place that's having bad weather. It's raining all over the South. I love going out in the rain, don't you, dear? Bad weather brings people together, you know. Makes them appreciate rainbows."

Nora smiled at the woman and squeezed the water out of her hair, pulling it into a tight knot at the back of her head. She looked terrible. There was no way she wanted that Bowles guy to see her like this.

"You wouldn't happen to have an extra ticket, would you, dear?" The little old lady reached into the pockets of her voluminous pink raincoat that nearly touched the floor. "I seem to have misplaced mine, and they tell me they're all sold out."

"I'm sorry, I don't," Nora said, thinking about the Bowles guy's ticket. Maybe he'd be gone by the time she got out of the ladies' room, and she'd never have to return it. Maybe he'd bought another ticket by now or found his friends. She only knew she didn't want him to see her looking like a drowned rat. She pictured his unforgettable face with those black brows, and that boyish grin that brought dimples to his cheeks; she remembered the way she felt when his hand touched hers. She tried to recall if his eyes were black or brown, and the sound of his voice. She reminded herself he was a stranger in town and probably looking for a one-night stand. "Men!" she muttered disgustedly, yanking her rain hat down over her hair. The little old lady smiled and came closer.

"It's difficult to find a good one nowadays, young lady. There *are* some left, though, I believe. You just have to beat the bushes."

Nora laughed into the mirror. God, she was wise, even if a bit flaky. "The bushes are over my head," she said. "It's a jungle out there!"

"I know, I know! But you must never give up, my dear. If you do, you might lose out on the man of your dreams. Your prince charming."

"I doubt that." Nora frowned skeptically.

"You never know, my dear. I had a good man once. Gus is gone now, but when he was alive he gave me anything my heart desired. Within reason, of course." She winked. "Oh, Gus had his faults, as all men do. But he was kind, good-hearted, and generous. A gentle man, if you know what I mean. If you ever find one like him, you must hang on tight and never let go." She laughed. "All relationships have their stormy weather, my dear. Like today. You're certain you don't have an extra ticket?"

It was as if she *knew* Nora had Alec's ticket in her pocket. "I'm sorry," Nora said, certain the little old lady knew she was lying. "But maybe—"

"Yes, my dear, what is it?"

"Would you do me a favor and look out the door to see if there's a man in a raincoat standing beside the phone booth?"

"Surely!" the old lady answered, scurrying instantly to the door to peer out into the lobby. "Yes," she whispered. "Tall and broad shouldered with blue-black hair and a glorious tan. Standing beside the phone booth like he's waiting for someone."

"That's him," Nora said, pulling her rain hat lower over her eyes. "This belongs to him." She handed the old lady Alec's ticket. "He lost it tonight when we met in the rain. Maybe if you return it, he'll give it to you." She smiled. "I hope so."

Chapter 2

THE STORM WAS worse by the time Nora found her seat on the aisle. Hail drummed on the roof and everyone looked up. She hoped the animals were safe at home. Her father's horse was afraid of lightning as much as she was. Beginning to shiver, she draped her hat over her legs, wondering if Alec Bowles had seen her leave the ladies' room. She didn't know why she was worried. She'd returned his ticket by way of the little old lady, unless the old girl hadn't given it to him. Of course she had. She shrugged, and water trickled down her neck from her wet head, disappearing between her breasts. Why was she wasting valuable time thinking about a stranger she'd never see again? She should be concentrating on the facts and figures about the farm and the shelter she wanted to build. This was her big chance, and she'd better be sharp.

The concert hall was packed, but that was understandable, considering that Zorowitz was playing. She eyed Eve's empty seat. She hoped her friend hadn't encountered any problems in the storm. The lights dimmed, and people stopped talking. "Standing room only for this performance," someone said. An usher approached her with a flashlight and asked if the seat beside her was taken. She nodded, wishing she'd stayed home with her dogs.

But Eve had insisted she come. She'd sat Nora down and put on her big sister act, convinced her the concert could be the solution to her pressing money problems. It had sounded like a great idea at the time. She loved Rachmaninoff. She loved Eve. They'd been best friends ever since they'd met in a piano store years before. They'd both wanted the same concert grand, the one Nora couldn't afford. Eve had bought the piano and invited Nora over to play it anytime she wanted. Nora had been a student then, going to school in New York and seriously considering a career in music.

And so it had been arranged. Eve had discovered a rich woman in Atlanta who'd helped save the zoo, some millionaire's widow who had bushels of money and loved Russian music and cats. Nora envisioned the shelter she'd wanted to build for strays since she was a little girl.

"Pardon me, is this seat taken?" a man's voice asked.

Shaken from her dreams, Nora looked up into the semidarkness and saw a beautiful face.

"It's me," he said, kneeling beside her in the aisle and flashing a smile. "Alec Knowles."

Him! Tiny goosebumps rose on her arms, and she felt her throat constricting. She was unable to speak, unable to breathe!

"Peachtree Street tonight in the rain." He touched her arm as if to awaken her from a deep sleep, and she let out a tiny gasp. "You gave me a ride, remember? I left my ticket in your van."

"But I gave it to a little old lady in a pink raincoat, and she promised to give it back to you. Didn't you get it?"

"I let her keep it for being so nice." He nodded toward

the front row where the little old lady in the pink raincoat waved and smiled.

"Oh," Nora said softly, realizing it sounded like a moan. She gave the little old lady a weak wave. "I'm sorry, but this seat's taken. My friend will be here any minute."

"I'll leave when he comes," he said, standing up and squeezing past her knees. Thunder exploded like bombshells outside, and hail bounced loudly off the roof, coming down so hard and fast that everyone began talking. The guest soloist pushed through the curtains on the stage and walked to his piano as everyone applauded.

"Only a frog strangler, huh?" Alec grinned, raising a brow and settling back into his seat. "I'd hate to see what a *real* storm is like in Georgia."

She gave him a little smile and uncrossed her legs, decided that was a mistake and crossed them again. Realizing he could see her shaking, she tried to relax by breathing deeply.

"Why didn't you tell me you were coming here?"

"Mr. Bowles—"

"Knowles," he said, touching her arm. "Alec."

"You'll have to leave."

"In the beginning of my favorite concerto? You must be kidding."

His favorite concerto! It was hers, too.

She looked at the grin on his face and wondered why this was happening to her. Why all the dogs and cats in the world followed her home. And men. She was forever trying to dodge some egotistical jerk who expected her to jump into his bed. Old men, young men, men with problems and one thing on their minds. Never a decent man. Never a prince charming. She smiled, recalling the little old lady's advice and telling herself to stay cool. No man was worth getting upset over, especially a good looking wolf on the make. But she was still alive and very much a woman, lonely and overflowing with love to give to a man. She rearranged her wet rain hat over her legs, accidentally hiking up her skirt as she observed Alec Knowles.

"You'll never get me to leave that way." He grinned and took in the view, raising a brow as she jerked her skirt down over her knees and stretched to see the stage.

"This concerto was written for making love," he said, leaning toward her. "In front of a fireplace on a rainy night like tonight."

She forced herself to stay seated, tempted to hit him with her purse. Why should she leave? To hell with him! She'd come to hear Rachmaninoff and save her farm. Ignore him and he'd go away. She felt his eyes wandering over her and looked down to see if her skirt was too high.

"You're really quite attractive," he said thoughtfully, in a low voice. "But why so tense? I'm not going to attack you, I promise."

"If you say another word, I'll call the usher," she said, looking him in the eyes, so dark and dreamy in the darkened hall that she thought she might faint. She seriously considered returning to her car and driving home. But she couldn't let down Eve or the animals.

"Your friend probably got caught in the storm." He patted her arm, seeming to sense her nervousness.

"Keep your hands to yourself." She pulled away, and he laughed in genuine amusement, lifting a brow and settling back into his seat to listen to the music. She listened too, closing her eyes and trying to contain her temper. Eve would be there soon, and the man beside her would leave, and she'd never see him again. She hadn't come to Atlanta for this. The trip was strictly business, and she mustn't forget it. Not even for the best looking male she'd ever seen!

"You're awfully quiet," he observed.

She held her head high, refusing to listen, refusing to look. She cleared her throat, leaning into the aisle and trying to cross her legs. Eve was right when she said all men thought about was sex. But why was *she* thinking about it lately? Was it because she was approaching thirty and about to reach her sexual peak? Maybe she was working too hard, or had lived in the woods too long, or shouldn't have given up men. She thought of Doug and knew she'd been stupid to believe all his lies.

Alec Knowles was staring at her. "You probably got chilled walking in the rain," he said quietly. "I feel responsible. We've got to get you out of those clothes and into a warm bed."

That was it! She stood up without a word.

"Wait!" he said, rising with her. She took long strides up the aisle, relieved just to be moving. For a while she'd thought he was almost nice, but he was like all the others, interested in a one-night stand. Feeling his hand on her shoulder, she increased her pace.

"I didn't mean what you think," he said, trying to keep up with her. People sitting in the aisles had to move aside for them.

She remembered Eve telling her she'd have to change, be more feminine if she ever wanted a serious relationship again. A tear slipped from her eye, and she wiped it away with her sleeve, realizing that the suit she was wearing was out of style and that her hands were red and rough.

"Nora!" Eve called as Nora entered the lobby. "Nora!"

"Eve!" Nora rushed over to her friend. "I was worried . . . afraid you wouldn't come."

"Me, not come?" Eve laughed, giving Nora a big hug. "What happened to you? You look like you just swam in from Lake Lanier."

"I'm afraid it's my fault she's so wet," Alec said, coming up behind Nora. Nora took Eve's sleeve and pulled her aside.

"Don't you want to introduce me?" Eve whispered. "He's such a hunk."

"I don't know him," Nora said. "I couldn't find a parking space, and I had to walk three blocks in the rain. Look at me. How can I meet that rich woman like this?"

"You'll have to," Eve said. "There's no time to get you dry clothes."

"You're welcome to use my hotel room," Alec suggested. "I'm at Peachtree Plaza downtown."

"I think I'd better go home," Nora whispered to Eve.

"Home? Are you crazy? We're supposed to meet Mrs. Finch during intermission. She's around here somewhere. I've never met her myself, but she shouldn't be hard to find. She always wears—"

"I can't meet her looking like this," Nora interrupted.

Eve held tightly to her arm. "What's wrong with you, kid? You know how important tonight is. Mrs. Finch is probably the richest woman in Atlanta. She could make the difference between saving your farm and building your shelter, or losing them altogether."

"She's wet and cold, that's all," Alec said in Nora's defense. "I couldn't help overhearing. I'd like to help, if I may. Here's the money I owe you for tonight, Nora."

"I thought you didn't know him," Eve said to Nora.

"Alec Knowles." He introduced himself with a melting smile. "It's my fault your friend is so wet. She did me a great service tonight."

"I don't want your money," Nora said. "I told you I don't charge."

"I think I missed something," Eve said.

Alec grinned at Nora. "You really shouldn't do it for nothing, you know. You're too good. Maybe you should go into business and raise the money you need that way."

"I'm sorry I ever picked you up! I should have left you in the rain!"

"Are you two together?" Eve asked.

"Of course not!" Nora scowled.

"She's probably running a fever," Alec commented. "She's shivering, as you can see. We've been together all evening. We came in her van."

"He's the one who's sick!" Nora told Eve, taking her friend's arm and dragging her toward the ladies' room.

"But he seems so nice."

"I'd like to take you both to dinner," Alec said, following them. "A drink and some hot food would do wonders for her."

"I don't drink!" Nora turned her back on him.

"Why not be nice to him if he wants to give you money, kid? I think he likes you."

"Well, I don't like him."

"Shhh! People are staring. There's a little old lady coming this way, and I wouldn't be surprised if she asks us to leave."

The little old lady in the pink raincoat ambled across the red carpet of the lobby, a warm smile on her wrinkled face as she extended her hand to Alec. "Dr. Knowles," she said sweetly. "I see you found your young lady."

"Thanks to you," he said, graciously taking her hand.

"And I must thank you for helping me get my ticket, my dear," the old lady told Nora. "Dr. Knowles was kind enough to give me his, as you suggested he might. But then, he's such a darling, isn't he? Reminds me of my Gus, you know. He's promised to bring you to my house to dinner soon."

"He what?" Nora said, not closing her mouth.

"Do you ladies know Mrs. Finch?" Alec asked, raising a brow.

"Mrs. Finch of Atlanta?" Eve asked, wide-eyed.

"Do I know you, my dear?"

"Eve Olson." Eve smiled, pinching Nora and shaking the little old lady's hand. "I've spoken with you several times on the phone about my friend here. Nora Flynn, remember?"

"Of course." Mrs. Finch smiled. "We met in the ladies' room." She took Nora's arm and whispered in her ear: "You'd better hang on to this one, my dear. He's just the sort of man I was telling you about earlier, and eligible doctors are hard to find."

"Eligible doctor?" Eve repeated, lowering her head to gaze over her glasses as Alec wandered off toward the phone booth. She took Mrs. Finch's arm and spoke tactfully. "I'm having a party at my house this weekend for Nora's animals, Mrs. Finch. An Adoption Party like the ones they have at the zoo. I hope you'll come."

"Oh, I love parties." Mrs. Finch smiled. "May I bring

my friend, that handsome Dr. Knowles?" Her gray eyes twinkled beneath sparse silver brows. "He's dreadfully charming, don't you agree?"

"He certainly is!" Eve gushed.

"I've invited him to stay with me while he's in Atlanta, and he's accepted, isn't that wonderful?" said Mrs. Finch. "He's only in town for reassignment, poor boy, and he hasn't seen much of our southern hospitality."

Eve smiled mischieviously, and Alec returned to hand Nora a check. "I've added a little tip for the extra . . . favor." He grinned.

"I don't want your money," Nora said, stepping back.

"Of course you do, my dear," Mrs. Finch advised. "It would be bad manners not to accept a Northerner's check. The doctor wants to help. It's for the animals, you know." She winked at Alec. "I believe I'll go home now. The storm seems to be over and I'm rather tired."

"I'll call a taxi," Alec offered.

"Thank you, my dear."

"Good night, ladies," Alec told Nora and Eve.

"Good night," Eve said softly, watching him go with a dazed expression on her face. "I thought you didn't know him, Nora Flynn. And Mrs. Finch? What's going on?"

"I picked him up on Peachtree like I would any helpless creature, and I met the old lady in the ladies' room. How was I to know who she was?"

"You can tell me about it later, my friend. Let me see that check."

They looked at the check together and couldn't believe their eyes. "Five hundred dollars!" Eve said at last. "Some pickup!"

"I can't believe it," Nora said softly.

"Five hundred dollars for picking him up, and Mrs. Finch likes him. Do you realize what we have here, kid?"

"What?" Nora asked blindly.

"We've got to make plans!"

"What kind of plans?"

"Plans for you and the doc, silly. He likes you—don't ask me why, you certainly treated him like the dog catcher."

"He isn't interested in *me*, Eve. All he wants is someone to share a bed with while he's in Atlanta. His check will probably bounce."

"Then go to bed with him, kid," Eve whispered. "I'm your friend, and I know what you've been through. Just think of your animal shelter."

The shelter roared through Nora's mind like a flying ark, floor, walls, roof, fences, kitchen, and grooming room. Then she saw Alec Knowles's face, his eyes, his dimples, his sensuous mouth. It might be fun playing a man's game for a change. Turn about *was* fair play, wasn't it? But she couldn't change her moral values. "Do *what* exactly?" Nora asked.

Eve slipped her arm around her friend's neck. "You are in a rut, aren't you, Nora? Just because you've given up men doesn't mean you have to give up sex."

"Would you care to explain that?"

"Come on, kid. I'm not trying to be cruel. I want to see you happy. You're not the only woman who's been wronged by a man. You're a member of an international club, and the membership's growing. I know what a rat your ex-boyfriend was. Now's your chance to get even. You can play *their* game. Who knows? You might win."

"I'm sorry, Eve, but you've got the wrong girl. I'm not into revenge."

"Okay, but where's your spirit? Where's Nora Flynn the fighter, the defender of helpless animals, the woman who has thirty days to pay back her boyfriend or forfeit her farm? You told me once you'd do anything short of murder to build NORA'S ARK."

Nora imagined she saw her ark sailing away on the clouds, filled with sad-eyed dogs and cats, a furry face in every window. She *did* have to raise one hundred and

fifty thousand dollars to pay devious Doug back. It might
be pleasant seeing the hunk again. As long as she didn't
have to . . .

"I'm listening, but I'm not making any promises,"
she said.

"Great! We start with your hair. My beautician can
do wonders with a long mane like that. And your face
will be a piece of cake." Eve dug into her purse and
pulled out two credit cards. "Take these, kid. You can
pay me back later. Meanwhile, buy yourself something
stunning for the party, as long as it's tight and sexy."

"Eve . . ."

"That's my name, kid. And don't forget what happened to Adam. And he was more of a male than anything
in pants today. Smile, Nora Flynn. You're about to save
your farm from falling into the hands of the enemy and
build that shelter you've been talking about since I met
you. And all with the stroke of a pen. Mrs. Finch's pen!
I'm going to give a party Atlanta will be talking about
for years. And you're going to teach that gorgeous northern doctor what southern hospitality is all about."

Chapter 3

IT WAS UNSEASONABLY cold in Atlanta on the night of
the Adoption Party; the weatherman predicted severe
thunderstorms and dropping temperatures.

Eve lived in Stone Mountain, a park and community
located about thirty minutes from downtown Atlanta,
known for its magnificent houses and estates. The elegant
formality of Eve's contemporary residence was balanced
by one of the world's largest pieces of exposed granite:
Stone Mountain itself. The spacious house, made of rock
and wood, with wrap-around decks, pool, and pool house,
was the scene of many a fancy party, a place where
Atlantans flocked when they received a coveted invitation. Eve Olson owned a string of antique shops throughout the Atlanta area. She enjoyed making people happy.
She was an animal and music lover. Maybe that's why
Nora was her best friend.

Nora had helped Eve decorate the three floors of the
contemporary villa. Together they had found countless
antiques in condemned buildings and junk yards: a chan-

delier from an old plantation near Newnan, churchpews from a small church in Macon, a pink marble fireplace from a hotel in Gainesville, now burning brightly in Eve's upstairs library. Tonight a silver ice bucket filled with red tulips had been placed at the entryway of the house.

Nora adjusted the front of her long white evening dress, and studied herself in the stained glass mirror above the fireplace. The salesgirl at Neiman-Marcus had shown her the slinky creation that was tailored, yet perfect for evening.

"I love the back, or lack of one," Eve commented, fastening two tiny buttons at Nora's neck.

"You're sure it's not too—"

"Sexy?" Eve laughed, watching Nora stand straight as a Georgia pine in an attempt to keep the V neckline from revealing the swell of her breasts. "It's about time you showed off that centerfold figure, Nora Flynn. Play your cards right tonight and you'll be moving those dogs and cats and rabbits of yours into new quarters." Eve hugged Nora affectionately and spoke in a sisterly tone. "Relax, kid. Our star guests won't be here for a while, and I've got a dozen things to do. Be a good girl and stay hidden. I don't want anyone seeing you until the last minute. I've got a great entrance planned."

"Entrance?"

"Yes, you'll love it. Just be yourself and remember your feed bill." Eve gave Nora a parting hug. "Read a book and listen to Debussy; he's on the stereo."

Be yourself... Nora considered Eve's words as she watched her friend slip through the open door, then pressed a button on the stereo. The music began, soft, melodious, and thought stirring. She went to the window and looked out at Stone Mountain in the distance, wondering how she could be herself when she felt so uncomfortable. It was raining steadily now, and she pressed her face against the cool glass as she listened to it coming down. She closed her eyes and saw herself growing old and lonely. It wasn't the life she wanted, but she'd accepted it. Animals couldn't hurt you the way men could. And she'd promised herself she would never be hurt by a man again.

She wandered back to the desk and lay down her little white bag, staring in the mirror with knowing eyes. "He's only a man," she murmured out loud. "Forget the past. It doesn't matter anymore. Nothing matters but your four-footed friends, and they're counting on you." Her neatly plucked brows arched over thick lashes, and her glossed lips glistened as they curved into a smile. Her hair was a new length, lightened and brushed back at the sides to show off pearl earrings. She hadn't looked this good since that night in New York after her recital, the night it had stormed and she'd come home unexpectedly and caught Doug with that girl.

Taking a deep breath and feeling her waist tighten where it was cinched with a gold-beaded belt, she turned to view the deep slit in the back of her dress. "The party will be over before you know it," she told herself.

Something moved behind her, and she let out a tiny gasp, spinning around on her heels as a man's hand grasped the back of the leather chesterfield sofa. Alec Knowles frowned attractively and arched a brow over the couch's humped back, his eyes heavy with sleep. Clearly, he'd been asleep on the sofa and had woken up just in time to hear her muttered soliloquy.

"Do you always psyche yourself up before a party?"

"How long have you been there?" she demanded. The cleft in his chin was more pronounced above an open shirt, which revealed a dark-haired chest.

"Long enough to know you're scared," he teased. He ran a hand over his mussed black hair and settled his lips into a sullen curl. "Now that's what I call a great looking dress. Anything beautiful always looks better in white. And that perfume! You smell so good I had a dream." He chuckled low in his throat. "A rather exciting one too."

His grin infuriated her, and she turned back to the windows, looking down on the lighted pool and pool house through the rain. "Does Eve know you're here?"

"I doubt it. The lady wasn't around when I arrived.

I had a rough night and came over early. I didn't want to disturb Mrs. Finch before the big party." He lit a cigarette and took a long drag, observing her through the thin haze of smoke and standing up to tuck his white shirt into his pants. "I talked to Eve on the phone, if that's what you're worried about. She said the door would be open, so I walked in. I found the library and sat down to read a book. I guess I fell asleep."

"Uh-huh," she muttered as a big gray striped cat meowed and paraded through the open door with his tail in the air, then jumped onto the couch with Alec.

"Hey, where did you come from, my furry friend?" he asked the cat. "You're soaking wet. I hope you have a better story than I did for the lady."

"He was probably out carousing, like you," she said, bristling. "You tomcats are all alike. I found Roy Bean here a year ago, tied in a tree where some mean boys were about to hang him. He nearly died, but he hasn't learned his lesson. He takes off every time the door opens."

"Maybe he's smitten with a pretty pussycat." Alec chuckled.

"Is that all you think about?" She picked up the cat and held him in her arms. Roy swiped her chin affectionately with a wet paw and purred.

"Does a guy have to be a beast to get along with you?" Alec came toward her slowly and stubbed his cigarette out in an ashtray on the table between them, looking at her with a warm gaze, as though he were looking right through her dress. His expression was unmoving, and her temperature rose, as he came closer until he towered over her, and the air between them sizzled. "Just who the devil are you mad at?"

"Don't touch me," she warned, holding the cat to her breast and stepping back.

"Take it easy, Nora. I'm not going to do anything. I don't know what is wrong with you, but I'd like to help, if you'd let me. Why don't we lie down and talk about it?"

His charm was turned on full force, and she tried not to lose her nerve. She thought about her animals and the party that would raise the money to pay the bills, about the dogs and cats and rabbits she expected to place in new homes, about Mrs. Finch and all her millions; she thought about why she *had* to be nice to him.

"I'm sorry, I'm a little nervous." She smiled sweetly. "This has been a rough week." She put Roy Bean down on the Grecian rug, knowing Alec could see her breasts, then moved slowly to the desk. "As long as you're here, I have something that belongs to you." She opened her purse and pulled out the check he'd given her. "I told you I don't charge for favors. Take it back, or I'll tear it up this instant."

"It's yours," he said calmly. He smiled, a warm goosebump-raising smile that made her tingle all over. "Use it for the dogs and cats. Whatever. You earned it."

"You gave it to me because you expected something in return. You deliberately embarrassed me in front of my friend."

"Oh, that." He laughed, walking around to view her from another angle, lighting a cigarette and placing his lighter on the table. "I'm not sure what I expected that night. I was just having a little fun. I thought you were some kind of a kook. Now I've changed my mind. You're serious about all this, aren't you?"

"Very serious, doctor." She tore his check in half and lay it on the table.

"Now what did you do that for? I gave you the money because I want to help. Take it easy. How about a cigarette?"

"I don't smoke."

"Good." He smiled and put his cigarettes away. "It's a bad habit, and I doubt you do anything bad, do you, Nora?" He didn't wait for her answer. "No, I'm sure you don't. I'm intrigued. New hairdo, sexy dress . . . talking to yourself. What's going on in that lovely head of yours? You can't blame me for being curious."

"What I do and how I dress is none of your business.

I don't have to answer to you. Not to any man."

"Oh, one of those?" He grinned, his velvety eyes gathering shades of red. "A liberated woman who doesn't wear a bra." His eyes bored through her dress, and her nipples grew taut as they pressed against the silken fabric. She returned his stare boldly, feeling tenuous and vulnerable and hating him because she was hating herself. He made her realize how much she missed being with a man, touching a man . . . being touched. She thought she'd outgrown the need, but she was wrong.

"Let's get something straight," she said shakily, looking up at him. "I don't give a damn what you think of me. I'm here to talk Mrs. Finch into building a shelter so a lot of poor dogs and cats won't have to die. I've got over a hundred animals depending on me tonight. If everything goes right, the dogs and cats and rabbits downstairs will eat again, and NORA'S ARK will be a household word in Atlanta tomorrow. Eve and I worked our butts off to get the right people to come here tonight, and I won't let anything you say spoil it."

His gaze fell downward to where her hips and buttocks curved into her dress. "Forget the animals for a minute. It's you I'm worried about. What a waste." He came closer, and she held her breath. His nearness was more than she could handle, and she didn't know what she'd do if he touched her. He reached out a hand, and she drew back instinctively.

"You've been spooked bad." He sounded puzzled, compassionate, and genuinely concerned. "You're afraid of me, aren't you, Nora? You're afraid of men!"

The door opened slowly, but neither of them noticed, their eyes locked in a wordless confrontation neither of them understood.

"I thought I heard voices in here," Eve said. "I'm glad to see you two are talking. Hey, what do you think of my new maid? Isn't she cute?"

Nora blinked, tearing herself from Alec's tough but tender gaze, looking out of the corner of her eye at the hairy brown hand Eve was holding. "A chimp!" she exclaimed. Eve coaxed a young chimpanzee through the door. "Where on earth did you find it?"

"Her!" Eve bubbled. "That's my surprise. She's an escapee from Markey's Primate Center. You know, the lab where they do all those horrid tests in the name of mankind. I got a call at two this morning saying that the police were out looking for her. The *Lovers of Animals* tried to reach you, but you weren't home, of course. You were here, sleeping peacefully in my bed. I didn't want to wake you, so I called Alec. Thank goodness I had his number. He offered to go looking for the chimp and stayed out all night in the rain. He found her this morning before daybreak." Eve turned to Alec. "Tell Nora where you found her."

"You tell her."

"In an outhouse!" Eve laughed. "A backwoods outhouse, sitting on the little kid's seat. Isn't that hilarious? She was scared to death, poor thing. But I gave her a bath and tied this apron on her. Adorable, isn't she? But we've got to be careful. The TV said the police are still searching for her."

Nora held her hand out to the chimp, who was wearing a little white apron and maid's cap. The female ape jumped into Nora's arms and wrapped its hairy legs around her waist, cuddling like a baby. "Anyone who would experiment on something this dear is a rotten creep," Nora said.

"Sometimes it's necessary," Alec said.

"I've dubbed her Twila," Eve added quickly. "What do you think, Nora?"

Nora looked at Alec, wanting to ask him what he meant exactly, what he thought about animal research. But there wasn't time, and this wasn't the place. "Perfect," she said, petting the chimp and holding her close.

Roy Bean meowed and jumped up on the table to get a better look at the chimp, stretching to reach Twila's foot with his soft paw.

"I'll go down and tell the TV people they can't take any pictures of the chimp," Alec said, preparing to leave.

"Thanks, Alec, I don't know how we managed before you came along." Eve waited until Alec was out the door, then turned to Nora. "That man makes me understand sheer lust for the first time in my life," she whispered.

"What do you suppose he meant?" Nora asked.

"About what?" Eve said, petting Twila's head.

"You know, what he said about using apes for research."

Eve made a face. "You ought to know how doctors think by now. What I want to know is what you two were talking about."

Nora couldn't get Alec's remark out of her mind. Was she really afraid of men? "Nothing," she said.

"Nothing?"

"I don't remember, Eve. We talked, that's all."

"Not about how to feed an orphaned skunk, I hope!"

"He said he liked my dress."

"Hey, now we're getting somewhere. What else?"

"I think he's suspicious."

"Well, make him *un*suspicious! We need him to get to Mrs. Finch. Run your fingers through his hair, hold his—"

"Eve!" Nora frowned.

"Well," Eve laughed, "I'd know what to do with a hunk like that."

"I wish I did," Nora said, shaking her head.

The Adoption Party should have been a complete success. Eve's sparkling crystal and silver looked beautiful against spring flowers in every color imaginable. The house overflowed with hospitality and painstakingly prepared food. Uniformed waiters in scarlet coats and buff-colored breeches carried trays of drinks and hors d'oeuvres for the two- and four-footed guests, while scores of Atlanta's best-heeled residents poured through the doors for the most unique party of the year. Dogs and cats wandered freely, dressed as clowns and hobos, wearing hats, jackets, and finery. Rabbits of several varieties, their ears encircled in garlands of flowers, each one wearing a different colored jacket, hopped across the plush Oriental rugs and chewed the long, expensive fringe.

Two champion Saint Bernards were dressed in evening clothes. The male, Nicky, wore black tie and tails. His wife, Myrtle, red-eyed and slobbering, showed off her flashy red and white fur coat to best advantage with a stunning gold sequined gown, which was fitted over her rump to disguise her long flowing tail. The Saints were the only *valuable* residents of NORA'S ARK, and Nora was determined to have them adopted by the person who would attract the most publicity—the governor himself.

The mayor and governor arrived together, greeted by a brace of mutts in hobo's rags, their eyes shining as they stood on hind legs.

The evening continued beautifully until a red Doberman dressed as a ski bum got excited and left a smelly trail in the dining room. What could you expect from a ski bum? There were bound to be a few accidents—only some of the animals were housebroken—but Eve didn't care.

By the time the grandfather clock in the downstairs hall thrust both hands upward, most of the guests had pledged their support by signing their names to adoption papers. Most, but not all. Nora explained at least a hundred times what it meant to adopt a stray. The party was designed to attract publicity, but every dog, cat and rabbit there was up for adoption.

She smiled and continued to talk, trying to look and act her best, trying to make friends for NORA'S ARK. She exhausted herself bringing dogs and cats to the back of the house, where helpers from the *Lovers of Animals* group slipped them into exercise pens. When she finally talked the governor into adopting the Saint Bernards, Nicky and Myrtle, she was beginning to droop. It had been a long week filled with preparation, including bathing, grooming and fitting for costumes all the dogs, cats, and rabbits. Thank goodness it was almost over.

The two Saints slumbered peacefully beneath the table

where Nora had set up her work area, Myrtle snoring like a bulldog with her head draped across Nicky's rump. Nora had promised to bring the two dogs in person to the governor's mansion one day that week for TV and newspaper interviews. Dozens of animals still needed homes.

Roy Bean, the tomcat, purred loudly on Nora's tablet as she attempted to write down a woman's name and address. Roy, dressed in a cerise velvet jacket and lavender bow tie, had been hamming it up all evening. Most of the animals enjoyed dressing up; the others tolerated it. Everyone admired Roy Bean because he was such a big handsome cat who looked like a tiger. Roy could have been adopted several times that night, but Nora was saving him for someone special.

The woman standing in front of Nora's table, wrists and fingers banded in emeralds and diamonds, was dressed entirely in green silk and feathers. "I'm here to adopt a bird," she told Nora. "I understand they're free."

Nora explained how the adoption procedure worked. No animal was free. She needed money to carry on her work, to feed and shelter the animals. In the winter they needed heat; in the summer they needed air-conditioning. Animal feed was very expensive. And veterinarian bills were skyrocketing. Some animals were sick when she found them. Some were injured and had to stay in veterinarian hospitals for months. Nora never put an animal to sleep. She couldn't kill anything. She had been defending animals since she was a child.

"All I ask is that you spare a few dollars a week so a dog or cat or horse can be cared for on my farm," Nora told the woman. "You'll be adopting a pet, but it will continue to live with me. Your name will go in our big book of donors, and the animal will be cared for all its life."

"But I want a parrot!" the woman exclaimed. "Big and white like the one on that show with the cute detective who chases criminals. Male and talkative to keep me company at night. With long silky feathers and a good sense of humor."

Nora wanted to scream. "People don't usually abandon birds," she said. "Especially expensive parrots. We get more of the common four-legged castoffs. The kind that bark and meow and don't like birdseed."

"Are you telling me I can't adopt a parrot?" the woman screeched in a high voice.

Roy Bean rubbed himself against Nora's face and meowed. "Excuse me, my cat has to go to the bathroom," Nora said. "If you don't mind, I'll just go and help him." She stood up with Roy in her arms. The woman's eyes grew so large, Nora thought they might pop out of their sockets.

"Well, I never!" the woman huffed, her loud voice waking Nicky.

The Saint sat up, lifting his huge head and yawning. Then he stood up and stretched ... and lifted his hind leg ...

"Oh, my God!" the woman howled, jumping away. "He peed on my dress! He peed on my dress!"

Nicky's ears went straight up, and he skidded across the floor in his hurry to escape. The woman's screeching woke Myrtle, who leaped off the floor and dove under the glass coffee table, where Nicky was hiding.

"Bad dog!" Nora said to Nicky. The coffee table teetered on Nicky's back, and cocktail glasses went crashing to the floor. Alec grinned at Nora from behind a bank of ferns.

"Did someone get bit?" someone asked.

"No," Nora smiled. She asked the woman to come with her to the ladies' room, where she would splash cold water on her dress.

"Are you crazy?" the woman screeched. "This is a DiVinchy! I bought it at Saks!"

"Please calm down," Nora said, looking anxiously

toward Alec for help. He came toward her with a drink in his hand, screwing up his face because the woman was yelling so loud.

"Come along, darling," he said to Nora. "It's time we went to bed."

"What about my dress?" the woman screeched.

"Send us a bill." Alec took Nora's arm and hurried her along. Nora held tightly to Roy Bean and smiled as Alec slipped his arm around her waist, drawing people's stares. "Excuse us," he said as they moved through the crowd of onlookers.

Nora followed Alec out of the central part of the house into another wing, past the old grandfather clock and up the stairs to the library. She didn't know why she felt so weak. Probably because she hadn't eaten all day and it was now past midnight. She was too tired to eat, too tired to think. Maybe if she'd stayed cool and reasoned with the woman in green, she could have talked her into adopting a rabbit. Oh well, the woman wouldn't have listened anyway.

How was she going to get all the money she needed, Nora worried. Mrs. Finch hadn't come to the party . . .

"Why the long face?" Alec tagged behind her up the stairs. "You should be smiling. I saw the governor sign up for the Saints. Think of the publicity you'll get. A reporter I was talking to told me he was going to play the story up big."

Alec was dressed in a tux, his crisp white shirt pleated down the front and black bow tie emphasized his manliness, his sexual allure. He carried his drink and a lit cigarette, closing the library door neatly with his foot.

"How can I smile after what Nicky did to that woman?"

"The woman's an idiot. The dog deserves a steak. Remind me to buy him one."

He stared at her, and she hoped to discourage whatever he had in mind. She walked quickly to the windows to see if it was still raining. Lightning flashed behind Stone Mountain and illuminated the sky. A breeze came up

from the Yellow River to sway the trees, and she thought
of her female cat, Lily Langtree, Roy Bean's first love.
Lily had disappeared mysteriously the last time Doug
had come to the farm. Nora had no proof Doug had taken
the cat, but when she'd asked him about it, she'd known
from his answer that he was lying. Where Lily was, she
didn't know. But she believed the cat would return to
her if she was still alive. She prayed the white cat was
safe and out of the storm. Then she remembered what
Nicky had done to the woman's dress and smiled.

"It *was* funny, wasn't it?" she said to Alec. His eyes
caressed her face, and she realized she'd ignored him all
evening. She would have laughed if she didn't just then
remember Mrs. Finch's failure to show up that evening.

"I'm sorry she didn't come," Alec said. "I don't know
what could have happened. I called, but she isn't home."

Nora didn't want to talk about it. Listening to the rain
beat against the house and watching the way the wind
moved the trees, she felt numb. They were in for another
storm, and she was too tired and depressed to be scared.
Now she would lose the farm.

"Don't give up on her," Alec said. "She's eccentric
and has her own way of doing things." He tossed his
cigarette into the darkened fireplace. "Sit down and unwind. You take one end of the couch, and I'll take the
other. Come on," he coaxed, patting the sofa. "I've had
my rabies shots."

Nora saw the warmth in his eyes, which shone mag-
ically in the golden glow of a Tiffany lamp. He seemed
a comfortable presence now. She walked slowly to the
couch with Roy Bean in her arms and dropped into the
chesterfield's luxurious leather depths, laying back her
head. She tugged off her latticed sandals and heard the
familiar click of the stereo and the soothing strains of
Debussy.

"*The Afternoon of a Faun*," he said, sitting on the
arm of the couch at the opposite end. He was staring at
her again. "Appropriate for an animal lover." She tried

to block out the soothing texture of his voice and didn't reply, hoping he would say nothing more, knowing it wouldn't be long before he made his next move.

"I'm sure if we got to know each other, we'd find we have more in common than good music. I like company myself. Little restaurants, sleeping late, and getting up to a big breakfast, the mountains anytime of the year, travel, and of course indoor sports. All of which are best enjoyed with a lady. If you knew me on a more... intimate basis, we might..."

"Go to bed?" she said with reckless bravery.

"That would be nice." He chuckled.

She refused to look into his warm eyes, so deep and dark that she might drown in them. He made her feel feminine and beautiful and sixteen. Her blood raced, and she thought about what it would be like to sleep with him, to have his marvelous hands on her skin, to feel his breath caressing her ear, to be held in his arms and revel in the bliss she'd find there. There was no danger in fantasizing. Nothing would happen as long as she kept her head. She raised her lids, and his eyes were still there, making her quiver and shake, making her all shivery inside, making her want him. She turned away. Roy Bean was asleep in her lap, and she wished she didn't have to wake him. She bent down to pick up her shoes, and Alec was beside her in an instant, catching her hand and holding it tight as a clap of thunder reverberated through the house.

"Leave them there. I like you better with them off. With everything off."

"You're impossible!" She tried to pull away. Lightning flashed and thunder crashed so instantaneously that she let out a startled cry.

"You're shaking worse than that chimp was when I found her." Alec slid a comforting arm around her back. "She was scared to death, and so are you."

"I don't like storms," she admitted, breaking free of him and grabbing up her shoes. She moved across the room as thunder boomed, cracking so sharply that it shook the house. In the next instant the lights went out.

"Stay where you are," Alec said. "I'll find a match."

"I can see," she lied, sliding her bare feet forward over the thick Grecian rug and bumping into a table. She groped in the dark to find a candle and heard dogs barking downstairs. Nicky's throaty bark was followed by the high-pitched screams of the woman in the green dress. Roy Bean meowed in the silence and brushed against Nora's legs, making her realize how alone she and Alec were, separated from the rest of the party.

"Where are you?" Alec asked, making his way toward her in the dark. Unable to find a candle, Nora slid her fingers quickly along the wall to the window, her white dress almost aglow in the blackness. "I found you," he breathed, touching her bare back with his warm hand and making her jump. She shivered beside him. He smelled wonderful!

"Where's your lighter?" she asked.

"I don't know." His breath heated her neck, and his hands took her shoulders and turned her around so that his face loomed above hers, probing, hesitant, and unbelievably virile. His eyes were lost in the darkness, but Nora had no doubt of what they were asking. She twisted to avoid him and tripped over the rug.

"Tell me about it," he said, catching her arm and pulling her so close that her breasts were flattened against his hard chest. His head came down to hers, and she let out a slight sound, her mouth temptingly open as his lips claimed hers and her heart stopped. His kiss was moonlight and falling stars and katydids on a warm August night. His lips moved over hers, and the tip of his tongue awakened her innermost desires. She leaned into him, sensations of pleasure and fear and need spinning through her like thunderheads, together with hunger and loneliness and passion. She felt as weak as a mouse and her head fell back as if she'd had too much to drink. Alec wasted no time, his lips moving like heat lightning across a summer's sky. His mouth found the V of her dress and Nora's eyes closed as his caressing lips spread like fever between her breasts. He trailed kisses down her arm until she could hardly breathe, moaning as his tongue flicked hotly against her skin, and she slid her arms around his neck.

"Alec..."

"Nora, darling. Don't be afraid. I'd never hurt you, I promise." She moved backward like a sleepwalker, falling helplessly across Eve's large desk. Pencils and pens fell to the floor, and she struggled to right herself up. Alec found her and lifted her into his arms, drawing her close to his heart and holding her there.

"Please let me go, Alec. I've got to get back to my animals . . . the guests."

"Not until you tell me what's wrong. Tell me, Nora. Let it all out." His massive shoulders flashed black against the lightning that streaked in the window. Thunder crashed so loudly that she ran her arms around his neck and laid her head against his chest. His lips found hers, and she was surprised by their tenderness. Then they swept up her cheek like a feather to caress her closed eyes. He kissed her temple and brow, her ears, swept back her hair and kissed her nose and chin, her cheeks, her eyelids, her open mouth.

"You don't have to hide your emotions with me, Nora. I'm human, no matter what you think to the contrary."

She didn't believe him, even though she wanted to. Men were experts at lying to women. He couldn't be a mere human; he was too gorgeous, too good to be true. Her common sense quarreled with passion and lost. She trembled convulsively.

"Try to relax," he said softly. "I'll take my hands away, if that's what you want." He removed his hands from her shoulders, and she thought she would be ill. "There, is that better?"

Dear God, no! Now she felt abandoned like some poor dog dropped on the side of the road. She wanted him back!

"What the—!" Alec cursed and jumped around in the

dark, grabbing at his leg. Nora thought he was swearing at her.

"Excuse me, darling, but your cat just used my leg to sharpen his claws. Or does he carry a razor?"

She laughed. "I'm sorry. Where is he? I forgot he was here."

"Good, that means you're feeling better. Maybe you'll let me hold your hand now?"

She could see him bending down to rub his scratched leg and laughed some more, relaxing and thinking he was nice. She couldn't see the expression on his face and wondered what he was thinking. She closed her eyes. It was ridiculous to be afraid of him. She reached out her hand, and he grasped it, clasping his other hand over it.

"You have beautiful hands, Nora. You should take better care of them. You work too hard."

"I love my work."

"That's because you're making good use of your life. There aren't many people who care about the suffering of others, animals or otherwise." He bent down and kissed her hand, caressing her fingers with his lips. She tried to pull away, but he wouldn't let her. "Why don't we sit down where we'll be more comfortable?" She shook her head. "No? That's okay, Nora. I don't mind standing up all night."

She laughed, surprising herself. He kissed her hand again, his lips lingering. "Please," she said.

"Why not? Don't you know kisses are the best remedy for sore hands?"

"Are they that bad?"

He found her arm, and slid his hand down until he found her other hand. "Now, that I'm holding both of them, no, they're not as bad as I thought. You have lovely hands, Nora. Small and feminine with long fingers. Strong, yet fragile. A woman's hands tell a lot to a man. I'll bet you didn't know that, did you?"

She laughed again. "Now I really wish I could see

your face. Where did you pick up that line?"

"No line," he said. "Some women don't do anything
with their hands but take care of themselves. Dress themselves, feed themselves, pamper themselves, touching
no one but themselves every day, every night, all their
lives."

"I never thought about it."

"Most people don't. We were given hands to help
others, to make things better, to make things happen, to
make things last. To reach out, to touch, to mend, to
heal . . . to love."

Nora's heart warmed. His words touched her. She'd
never known a man like him, never heard a man talk
that way. Had she misjudged him? He was tugging on
her hands, and she warned herself to be careful.

"Come here, Nora," he said. "Please." She took one
step forward, then another. "My hands won't hurt you,
Nora. I only want to make contact. Do you mind?" She
would have minded before. Now she didn't. His fingers
touched her chin lightly and tilted her head back. "Fingertips are the most sensitive part of the body, Nora.
Can you see me?"

"No."

"Then touch me, Nora."

"I can't."

"Why not?" She couldn't tell him she didn't trust
herself. It had been a long time since she'd touched a
man, really touched . . . She knew herself too well. She
wasn't like the women he'd described, the ones who
enjoyed touching themselves. Thank Heaven for that!
She enjoyed touching—people, dogs, cats, animals—
reaching out for love, wanting to be loved in return. It
had been a long time since a man had loved her. A very
long time.

She reached out blindly and touched his chest, raising
her hand slowly until she felt his neck, his adam's apple,
the rough stubble of a beard beneath his chin, his square
jaw, his silken lips . . .

"There." He chuckled, as if with pleasure. "Was that so bad?"

"No," she said, withdrawing her hand.

"Not so fast. You've just begun." He grasped her hand gently by the wrist and drew it back to his face, touching her fingertips to his smooth cheek. She felt the deep creases of his dimples, which were always there because he smiled a lot. His face fascinated her. She felt him turn his head, and then his mouth pressed into the palm of her open hand.

His kiss made her close her eyes as tremors of delight rippled downward through her breasts, over her rib cage, her hips, and settled between her legs. His mouth found hers, and her lips parted gently as his tongue foraged. She found herself yielding, clinging, returning his kiss fervently, unable to help herself, unable to stop. Roy Bean meowed and rubbed himself against her bare legs, forcing himself between her and Alec.

"Roy wants to get out," she murmured. Alec's hands slid down her back to her buttocks, pulling her close until she could feel the hardness of his rising passion. "The cat . . ." Alec closed her mouth with a kiss, deeper and more insistent, the touch of his tongue on hers sending exquisite sensations throughout her body, stirring her, exciting her. Nora's mouth opened and the word "Roy" strangled in her throat. Alec held her in his arms and kissed her again and again, her face, her hands, her breasts. "Please . . ." she gasped.

"Nora, darling."

"I've got to take Roy out."

He grasped her arms. "Can't he use the fireplace?" She was trembling so badly she couldn't answer. She knew he was shaking too.

"No. And if I don't go with him, he'll run off. Someone will open a door, and he'll be gone."

"So, let him enjoy himself." He kissed her open mouth, his tongue tracing the line of her teeth.

"You don't know Roy," she said, returning his touch.

"If there's another cat around, he'll stay out all night. He could get into a fight."

"Hmmm," he said, caressing her lips with his. If he didn't stop, she wouldn't be responsible for what happened. She kissed him back, little kisses that became increasingly passionate. His breath seemed hotter, and she leaned into him like a tree in a storm. "Roy's a tomcat. He can take care of himself," he said.

"I can't take the chance." She took a deep breath and headed blindly out of the room, bumping into a wall and seeing stars.

"Nora, are you all right?" He was at her side kissing her neck, slipping his fingers inside the slit in her dress, caressing her back with his lips, breathing against her bare skin and making her shiver. "Don't go, Nora. Not now."

If she didn't go, they would make love. She couldn't chance that. She took great gulps of air and stumbled forward. She found the door, the knob.

"Don't go, Nora. Not when we both want—"

"Please, Alec." She removed his hand from her arm as gently as she could. "Don't say it."

"Nora." He drew her back against his chest, sliding his arms beneath her breasts, burying his face in her hair. He held her close until Roy meowed, as if saying goodbye, and slipped through the door.

"Roy!" Nora called, pushing Alec's hands from her breasts and rushing into the dark hallway as if she'd just found her way out of a maze. Meowing, Roy Bean ran down the steps in front of her. "Roy!" she called, tripping down the plushly carpeted corridor. What was wrong with her? She leaned against the wall to keep from falling, feeling intoxicated although she hadn't had a drink. What had Alec done to her?

Eve met her at the bottom of the stairs, carrying a candle. "Nora, I've been looking everywhere for you."

"What's wrong?"

"Twila's gone. She got out the door somehow when the lights went off, and ran away. Someone said he saw her heading for the pool house. Where's Alec? The little thing knows him."

"I'll go," Nora volunteered, rushing to the French doors as a means of escape from Alec. She pushed the doors open against the wind and went out onto the deck into the pouring rain.

"Wait, Nora!" Eve shouted as thunder exploded. "Don't go out in this storm!"

Nora ran along the length of the deck until she found the steps and hurried downward in a daze. She glanced dizzily back at the house as lightning lit her way, wind whipping through her hair like eerie fingers. The manicured lawns spread out like a green carpet, drenched geraniums lined a brick walk leading to the pool house some distance away.

"Nora!" a voice called from above as she reached the lower deck and lightning tore the sky in two. Terrified that she'd be struck by lightning, she screamed when a branch fell from a tree and landed in front of her. The grounds were lit like the Fourth of July, and tall pines whooshed above her head. Running now, she raced along the brick walk to the pool house, sliding on the slick bricks as she passed the pool and climbed the steps to the door. Hail pounded on her head and collected in the back of her dress, making her shiver violently. She pulled open the pool house door, slammed it shut behind her and leaned against it, panting.

The storm raged on the other side of the wall of glass that faced the pool, but she was safe. If she stayed in the pool house until the storm was over, everyone would be gone, including Alec.

Her emotions flooded her mind. She'd wanted Alec to kiss her back in the library. She'd wanted him. Him!

Her eyes caught something hanging from the ceiling, and she raised her head. A black shape seemed to fly across the rafters of the exposed-beamed room.

"Twila!" The red-brown ape grabbed the chandelier and hung by one long hairy arm. "You almost gave me a heart attack, you hairy ape. Come down here!"

Twila obeyed instantly, dropping like a bag of sand on Nora's head. With a grunt Nora fell back against the door, and Twila chattered wildly.

"Yes, I'm alive, no thanks to you," Nora said. "Do you have to play so rough?" Twila wrapped her arms around Nora's leg and whimpered and hooted like a frightened child. Nora's head ached where the chimp had struck her full force, and the door moved behind her.

"Nora, are you all right?" Alec slipped inside the room, his clothes drenched. Thunder sent Twila crawling into Nora's arms to bury her head in Nora's wet hair.

"You found her!" Alec exclaimed. Nora held Twila close, trying to ease the young chimpanzee's fears, trying to lessen her own.

"She found me." The electricity came on, and Nora saw Alec's face from the pool lights outside. He looked into her eyes, burgeoning impatience creasing his brow. He came closer and she stepped back, his hand touching her arm.

"Do you think she would allow you to put her down?" he asked.

"No." Twila was her shield now. He couldn't do anything as long as she had the chimp.

"Maybe she'll come to me?" He closed in on her, stroking Twila's head and neck, her arm. Twila turned her head a little and peeped at him. The young ape's eyes shone with fear and innocence. "Twila, darling," Alec said softly. The chimp reached out a hand to him, laying her head on Nora's shoulder and making monkey sounds. "She's only a baby," he said. "Not quite two, from the looks of her."

"How do you know?"

"I used to work with primates."

"Where?"

"In Africa."

That made sense. Twila held onto Nora's neck as Alec continued petting the chimp, talking softly and taking the chimp's hand, running his fingers down the curve of her spine to her bare pink rump. Nora remembered how he had touched her in the library. She laughed softly and Alec moved closer.

"What's so funny?"

"You, doctor. First you make love to me, and now Twila. I knew you were a wolf, but this is too much!"

"I like females," he teased, moving closer and touching her arm at the same time that he stroked the chimp's breast. He bent down to kiss Nora's bare shoulder, and she realized how wet he was.

"You're soaked through," she said, staring at his dripping hair, as black and wet as a Georgia river bottom. His bangs flicked over his forehead as they had that night on Peachtree Street. He overwhelmed her.

"You're soaked too." As he gazed into her eyes, she saw a reflection of her own yearning. She watched, fascinated, as he stroked and petted the chimp and her, caressing, kissing, making love to her with his hands and eyes, his lips, his body. She wanted him, there was no doubt about it. If only she knew what he was thinking, what he was planning next. She couldn't deny the attraction she felt for him. It was like nothing she'd ever known with a man. But she would never suffer for love again.

A flash of lightning and a crash of thunder made the lights go out again. "Alec!" Nora moved against him.

"Nora." Her heart soared.

"We'd better sit this one out, darling. Come along." He slid an arm around her back, and his warm hand made her close her eyes. He helped her around a table, and Twila's head drooped onto Nora's chest. Nora sneezed.

"Cold?"

"A little," she answered.

He led her to where some old wicker furniture formed a circle, white in the darkness, the big pillows covered with chintz. Nora remembered the room now. She and Eve had had fun decorating it like a house in California they'd seen in a magazine. The fragrance from a crystal bowl of lilacs filled the air, and Nora's senses reeled. She loved flowers, and next to roses, lilacs were her favorite. Alec picked up a hand-crocheted afghan from the wicker loveseat in front of them and draped it over Nora's shoulders. He turned to look at Twila's face and chuckled.

"She's asleep," he said. "Lay her down on that big rocker, and we'll stack pillows around her." He took Twila gently from Nora's arms and settled her on a cushioned rocker. Nora watched in silence, observing this man who handled a chimp like a human baby, cradling Twila's head in his hand until he could slip a pillow beneath it. He stacked little pillows around the chimp so Twila would feel secure.

"Now that the cat is out and the baby's asleep, where were we?" he said.

Nora swallowed. "I'll stay with her. You can go back to the house. I know you have better things to do than sit with a monkey."

He frowned. "You must really think I'm a rat, Nora Flynn. What kind of man leaves his woman in a frog strangler?" He moved toward her, and her "buts" were lost in the explosive thunder that shook the pool house. "No buts, dearest," he whispered, taking her in his arms. Lightning lit up the house like daylight, revealing the determination in his gaze.

"Please, Alec," she whispered, eyeing him with distrust.

"Say my name again," he said. "I like the way it sounds. I like your accent, the way your mouth moves, the way your lips..." He was kissing her mouth then. Tenderly. His hands held her face, and his fingers slipped upward to her temples as his mouth tempted hers. "Kiss me," he said, touching his lips to her mouth and soothing her with the magic of his touch. She held her breath and tried to think. Her heart said to respond, but she didn't dare listen, fighting her heart like the wind against the roof. Alec's kisses mesmerized her as they drifted downward. That old familiar warmth spreading within her until it mushroomed between her thighs. Alec moaned, deliriously happy, and shifted slightly to kiss her breasts.

"Please, Nora, now I'm begging. I want you. Let me make love to you, please." Lightning flashed, and she was lost in the rapids of desire, a log in a swirling river of passion. Alec's kiss was sweet, and her reserves began to crumble. She was helpless in his arms. "I've wanted you since that first night on Peachtree Street," he murmured.

"You thought I was a man."

"Not after I saw your legs." His voice was filled with desire.

Accustomed to the dark now, she reached up to touch his face. The smile he gave her made her grab his shoulder to keep from falling. Her hand slipped around his neck, and he brought it to his lips to kiss her fingertips gently. Then he reached down and slid an arm beneath her legs, lifting her and carrying her with ease across the room.

"Where are you taking me?"

His face came down to hers and answered with a kiss. The perfume of rain and wet earth and lilacs filled the air with spring.

Nora was transported into a world inhabited only by the two of them. Alec pushed open a bedroom door with his foot, moving quickly to lay her gently on a white-sheeted bed with black bed hangings. The room was cool and secluded, with a fireplace and bath behind a mirrored pillar surrounded by baskets of white lilacs. As the storm raged outside, they entered a garden. Lilacs placed beside the bed in a crystal bowl emitted clouds of white fragrance. Alec sat down beside her, lifting her head to move a black and rust silk cushion beneath it.

"You've got to get out of those wet clothes, darling. You'll feel better when you're dry and warm." Nora shook her head as he undid the back of her dress, slipping the shoulders down over her arms one at a time. "Don't worry," he added, kissing her forehead, then her cheeks, her neck, her shoulders, little kisses that made her want him all the more. His hands lingered on her face—her eyes, her temples, her brows—stroking, caressing each inch of her until he reached her two full breasts. "You're beautiful," he said, lowering her wet dress to her waist and over her legs. "Simply beautiful."

Nora didn't believe him. She yanked a cool white sheet over her trembling body.

Alec began to undress, the epitome of unselfconsciousness, his dark chest broad and tanned and pleasing to her eyes. His stomach was flat and firm, and his maleness filled her with shocking desire. He looked at her, the light in his gaze reflecting the tempest that surged inside her.

"Nora, darling," he said softly as he joined her on the bed and kissed her cheek. He drew off the sheet and buried his face in her breasts. "I'd never do anything to hurt you, Nora." He held her close, and her hands spread across his broad back as she closed her eyes. His kisses raised her desire to a heady peak. She felt the bliss of a woman when a man holds her, loves her, his mouth raining kisses. She became feverish with desire, hearing the storm snap the trees, his voice whispering her name. Lost in the intensity of passion, she breathed the scent of lilacs and moaned with delight as Alec kissed every part of her, every curve, every hollow, every hungry erotic place. She moved beneath him and clutched his shoulders as his tongue traced a love line from her lips to her toes.

"Alec!" she whispered, trembling on the brink of ecstasy. Exhilaration, and then sheer abandonment followed as his hands took hers and showed her the way; thrilled, intoxicated, she was caught in the tempest that carried her. The pool house trembled too, as thunder crashed.

She sighed deeply, catching her breath, feeling like a woman again. He made her happier than she'd ever been. He held her in his arms and loved her, filling her with himself, making her proud to be the object of his desire, joining with her until it wasn't storming anymore, until it wasn't raining anymore, until it wasn't night anymore.

Chapter 4

NORA SAT IN the tub and lay her confused head back as the fragrance of lilac soap filled the air, transporting her back to the pool house the night before. Mere hours before, actually. She'd driven home in a daze, arriving at her farm before daylight. She didn't remember the more than fifty miles to Loganville. She only remembered making a fool of herself.

Now she must put Alec Knowles from her mind. But how? How could she forget a face like his, or the exquisite way he'd made love to her? She saw his dark eyes and smiled, recalling the way she'd untangled herself from his embrace, the look of sweet contentment on his face when she kissed him good-bye, the terrible sound of her footsteps when she left him behind.

Though she turned the water on full force, she still imagined she heard the rain pounding against the pool house roof, the thunder booming so loudly. She let out a tiny gasp. Roy Bean meowed and put his front paws on the tub to look at her. She scrubbed her face, trying to remember, at the same time trying to erase, all traces of Alec's kisses.

She turned off the faucets and slipped back down into the hot water, closing her eyes to feel Alec's strong arms once again beneath her breasts. Her eyes flew open, and she stared at the blue tiled wall in front of her, a feeling of guilt shattering her remembrances. A guilt so awful she could never wash it away.

Had she allowed Alec to make love to her because Eve had encouraged her to play up to him, intending to use him to get to Mrs. Finch? Had money become that important to her, so necessary that she'd betrayed her moral values and become like the men she despised?

"No!" she exclaimed, clapping her hands on the water so loudly that Roy Bean jumped up. She'd never meant to *use* Alec. She'd tried to get away from him, but he'd followed her to the pool house. What had happened after that hadn't been planned. It had happened, that's all. She didn't know why, only that it wouldn't happen again.

She pulled the plug from the old white tub and listened to the water chuckle as it drained out. Who was she kidding? Not herself. Alec made her deliriously happy, and fulfilled for the first time in her life. Was that how it was meant to be between a man and woman? Sweet and tender and so exciting that she would cherish the memory forever? She smiled, the remembrance of Alec's touch on her skin, his kiss, making her tremble once again.

She stepped from the tub, reaching for a fluffy towel and drying her face and hair. She patted herself dry and tossed the wet towel onto the edge of the tub, wrapping herself in a terry robe and heading for the sun deck at the back of the house. The sun was out for the first time in weeks, and it felt warm and delightful on her face. She removed the robe and sat down on a bench built into the deck, watching the horses chase each other in the pasture. She enjoyed the deck; it was her favorite place next to the spot where she planned to build her shelter, the place in the woods where birds sang and deer came to feed in the winter. She hadn't been in the woods for a long time now, not since Eve had told her about the concert and rich Mrs. Finch. Not since Alec. Now she'd have to find another way out of her dilemma. Mrs. Finch hadn't been interested enough to come to the party.

Nora tried to force the little old lady from her mind, as she did everything that made her unhappy. The sun felt so wonderful. She sat back and relaxed, watching a bee kiss a wisteria bloom. If only things had been different between Alec and her. If only they'd met before her life had become so complicated. If only they'd met another way, dated, fallen in love. Love . . .

Roy Bean meowed and jumped up beside her. She scratched the gray cat's ears. Of course there were other women in Alec's life. A man like him was bound to have dozens of females chasing him. It would have been nice to show him her farm and tell him about her plans. Silly! She shook her head and reminded herself she was almost thirty. Old enough to know about men and one night stands. Old enough to know she'd never see Alec again.

Her gaze drifted back to the pasture, where a wooden sign saying NORA'S ARK hung over the front gate. Her father had made the sign from a Georgia pine when she was ten, the day she brought home a starving dog and its nine pups. She could still recall the dog's face and prominent ribs. When she grew up she would help poor dogs and cats, she'd told her father. Don't forget, he'd said back, hugging her tight. She almost had forgotten. Until the night she broke up with Doug. The night she left New York and came back to Georgia to save the farm. The night she promised herself she'd never depend on a man again.

She watched the horses gallop along the fence. They only did that when a car was coming up the lane. No one came calling on Sunday, not since she'd hung the chain across the drive with the CLOSED sign in red letters.

The horses raced each other to the stable, and she was distracted by a chorus of howling dogs. The racket started in the main kennel and jumped quickly to the house.

Wolf, and Mincemeat, the half-breed bitch she believed
was Wolf's daughter, took up the mournful howl. The
sound of a car's motor was almost lost in the din of the
canine serenade. No point yelling and telling them to
shut up. No one would care. Not in Walton County,
where her closest neighbor lived two miles down a dirt
road and was deaf anyway. Besides, they'd stop in a
minute or two.

"Hello," came a friendly voice, masculine and ob-
viously amused. Not *him!* Not at seven in the morning
in the boondocks, when he was supposed to be asleep
in Eve's pool house on one of Stone Mountain's most
elegant estates. She covered her breasts with her hands
and dove for her robe. Roy Bean meowed in alarm and
jumped off the deck.

"I guess I have the wrong house." Alec chuckled. She
heard his footsteps on the gravel driveway, and the sound
of a car door opening and closing.

"We're closed!" she yelled in a desperate attempt to
make him leave. She heard him laugh, then nothing, and
waited breathlessly for the sound of his car's motor.

"Go in the house," he yelled somewhere behind her.
"I'm not going to look, although it's a terrible temptation
for a man so early in the morning."

"Go away!" she yelled, darting across the deck and
throwing open the screen door to run through the living
room to her bedroom. What was he doing here? She
couldn't see him again. Couldn't look at his face, his
eyes!

She tried to decide what to do, short of running into
the woods and hiding until he was gone. She went to the
mirror and ran a comb through one side of her hair. No
wonder the horses were excited. She'd been too preoc-
cupied thinking about him to notice he was driving up
her lane! She threw down the comb and looked at herself
in the mirror, finding a different woman staring back at
her than the one at Eve's house. This face was scrubbed
clean of makeup, plain and unpretentious. She pulled on
a pair of jeans, not pausing to find underclothes, and

shrugged into an old, oversized red cotton shirt. She tied it at the waist in a knot. It would have to do, she told herself, pulling her still-wet hair back into a ponytail with a blue scarf. She made certain she couldn't see through her shirt, deciding to get rid of him quickly.

He was standing on the front porch talking to Wolf, Mincemeat, and the six ugly, half-grown pups she'd found in a gully. Roy Bean meowed when he saw her and Alec looked up.

"I know, I know," she told the black cat, Smudge, who was crying for attention. She pushed open the screen door, ignoring Alec. "You want to get back to your kittens." The cat ran inside the kitchen, and Nora straightened up to look into the eyes of the man who'd made such glorious love to her only hours before.

"Good morning," he said in a voice that made her heart soar.

"Morning," she said, sauntering casually onto the porch and going to the other side. Keeping her back to him, she watched the horses lick a salt block.

"Why did you leave?"

"I'm sorry." She wrapped her arms around a cracked and peeling porch post. "I'm never myself when it storms."

"But you were wonderful!"

"We're closed Sundays." She let go of the post and eyed the dogs and cats that were waiting patiently to see what would happen next. "Most people rest on the seventh day, but it's just another work day for me. I have lots to do."

"I'll help you." He came toward her in his well-worn boots and faded denims, a blue shirt open at his throat to remind her of what she'd touched only hours before.

"Please go," she said, moving away from him.

"Not until I adopt a cat. The one I took a liking to was gone this morning; along with something else I thought was mine."

"We have plenty of cats," she said, looking him in the eye. "I doubt I have what you want, though."

"But you do!" He grinned. "Exactly what I want."

"This way, Dr. Knowles." She tried not to smile, but couldn't help herself. She went down the steps with Mincemeat, Roy, and Wolf, nervously twisting the knot in her shirt. "How did you find me?"

"Your friend, Eve. I was worried about you. When I woke up this morning, I found an ape in my arms. It was quite a shock. Especially when it kissed me."

She muffled a giggle at the thought of Twila puckering up. "That'll teach you never to toy with a monkey's affections." She regarded him in a businesslike manner. "If you'll excuse me, I've got dogs to worm."

"I'll help."

"I'm perfectly capable."

He took her arm and looked down at her. His face was even more wonderful in the sunlight, tanned and smiling and pure male. "I know, but I want to help, Nora. I want to do anything I can to give you a hand. You're doing wonderful work out here. Eve told me about it, and I know you don't have any employees."

"Did Mrs. Finch send you?"

"No." He shook his head. "I'm here on my own. But that doesn't mean she doesn't care. I talked to her on the phone this morning, and she sends her love. She likes you very much."

"Please don't get my hopes up again. I can't take another disappointment like last night."

"And I thought I made you happy." He looked deep into her green eyes, and she thought she'd collapse and roll down the hill to the barn. "Just goes to show you how wrong a man can be."

"Come on," she said suddenly, determined to show him where she planned to build her shelter. "I'm sorry about the high weeds, but I can't afford bush-hogging, and I'm too busy with the animals to keep the place looking like a park." He glanced at the marigolds planted in front of the barn. "The *Lovers of Animals* send me a volunteer on Mondays," she explained. "The rest of the week I'm on my own."

"What do you do on Mondays?"

"I go to Markey's Primate Center and give them a bad time. There's a lot of us who don't like what they're doing here in Georgia."

"You mean you don't like using primates for behavioral research?"

She nodded.

"I heard about the protests of pro-animal activists when I came back to Atlanta. But Markey's is doing some worthwhile experiments."

He knew a lot about Markey's, considering he was so new in the area. But he worked for the CDC, which had a branch in the same county as the primate center.

"We're determined to get the primates their rights . . . the right not to be experimented on at all."

"I doubt that will ever happen, Nora. Basic research will probably always require live animals. Especially if the study involves a disease, like cancer."

"Every animal used for research represents human failure," she said. "We want them to use alternate methods."

"But living organisms are so complex, Nora. Microchips and petri dishes won't ever completely replace live creatures as models for humans."

"You're like all the scientists who maintain a double standard when it comes to animals. They claim to respect animal life as long as it doesn't conflict with their needs."

"I'm opposed to using live animals for experimental purposes unless no alternative methods are available. But hundreds of thousands of people are alive because of heart and lung machines, cancer therapy, vaccines, insulin and many other advances in medicine, Nora, which were all made possible through animal experimentation."

"And all those people owe their lives to some poor animal who made those advances possible."

"I don't deny it."

She saw him in a different light now. He was a doctor, and most of them believed in using animals for research. She led him to the stable, feeling angry and anxious to be rid of him. He helped her across a narrow stream that

ran with clear bubbling water, but she pulled her arm
away. Two horses met them at the gate of the corral and
whinnied. Nora reached out her hands to stroke their
noses.

"Do you ride?" she asked Alec with a deceptively
sweet smile.

"A bit." He grinned and followed her through the gate,
where she caught a big black stallion by its halter.

"My father's horse," she said. "He's hard-headed like
an Irishman and likes to show off, but you can handle
him, I'm sure. He's really a cream puff."

"The cream puff's name?"

"We call him Ramp." She handed Alec a western
saddle and caught him admiring her behind. She gave
him a dirty look, and he grinned back, raising a brow
and watching her as she pulled herself up onto a pretty
gray mare with a star on her forehead. She wiggled se-
ductively in the English saddle, purposely goading him.

"Why did you leave this morning without saying a
word?" He held her horse's head and looked up at her
breasts beneath the thin gauze of her shirt.

"There was nothing to say," she answered, realizing
what he was staring at. She shook out her reins and stung
her mare's sides with leather, taking off like a bullet
before he could reply. Looking over her shoulder, she
saw Ramp dancing sideways. Wild-eyed, the horse laid
back his ears. Ramp would teach him about animals, she
thought. The skiddish stallion didn't like strangers, especially ones on his back.

Then Alec was in the saddle and flying through the
pasture's gate behind her. Ramp's hooves churned red
clay and took a short cut through a muddy field, slopping
wet mud on Alec's jeans. He swore at the horse and told
him to slow down. Nora reined in her mare and waited
for them to catch up.

"You're sure he's never run in the Kentucky Derby?"
Alec asked. Ramp trotted alongside the mare, and Nora
laughed, leaning down to touch her cheek to her mount's
mane.

"Why? You didn't have trouble staying on him, did you?"

"Not a bit." He squinted at her in the sun, his expression serious and confused. She raised her head and switched her mare with her straps, taking off for the woods and bending low as they crashed through thick brush and lacy pines. She heard Alec yelling at the horse behind her, swearing and pleading with it to slow down. She knew Ramp wouldn't let the mare out of his sight.

It was only a minute or two before Alec reappeared, having cleared a new trail through the woods. Ramp skidded to a halt beside the gray mare, and Nora broke out laughing.

"What's so damned funny?"

"You, on that horse. You're the first one who's ever gotten him out of the corral without landing on his behind."

"I have a feeling this is the real Nora I see," he said.

"Right, Dr. Knowles." She straightened her face. "The one at the party last night was a phony." She slid down from the saddle and petted the mare's head.

"And the pool house?" The questions in his eyes made her shiver. She held Ramp's bridle as Alec dismounted. He jumped down beside her and his breath warmed her hair, his dark eyes sparkling in the light.

"I'm impressed," she said, evading his question. "You rode Ramp like a pro. Evidently you're good at everything you do."

"I can't vouch for that." His eyes searched hers intently. "When a lady runs off and leaves a man without a word, he wonders."

"Last night was a mistake," she said icily. "I'd appreciate it if you'd forget it happened."

"Like hell I will. What kind of game is this?"

"I never planned to see you again, that's all."

"And women say men are cruel." The muscle flexed in his jaw, and his eyes took on fire. "I had every intention of seeing you, Nora. What did you think I was? Some stud who was out to make a record for himself?"

"You're only in Atlanta for a week. For reassignment."

"Maybe longer. I've been offered a job here. I'm seriously considering it. I like Atlanta. I like it more after last night."

He sounded sincere, but so had Doug. Why was he telling her this? Her feelings for him grew stronger with every breath; her heart pumped blood to her brain at a furious pace. Take it easy, an inner voice warned. He could hurt you bad.

"What kind of doctor are you?"

"An epidemiologist. A disease detective. I'm a surgeon too, but I have a yen for travel. I guess I should have been a pilot."

"My father was a pilot," she said without thinking.

"Did he have his own plane?"

"Yes." She looked away. "What do you do for the Center of Disease Control?" She wasn't sure she wanted to hear his reply.

"Travel mostly. I've been a lot of places." He smiled, evidently pleased by her interest. "Our assignments take us everywhere. I just got back from Africa."

"That explains the tan."

"Yes. I was in Kenya. I hated to leave."

"I'd love to see Africa." She wasn't angry now. "All those animals, it must be wonderful."

"It is. I'd like to show it to you someday."

She looked up at him with apprehension and distrust. He bent down and kissed her lightly on the lips.

She didn't mind a little kiss. But she suspected he wanted to pick up where they left off in the pool house. His lips were a heavenly shade of pink, warm and soft like the sunshine. He kissed her again, a better kiss, deeper and more lingering, his tongue touching hers as she felt her legs buckling.

"Doctor . . ."

"Alec," he said, wrapping his arms around her and

making the morning wonderful, his breath tickling her cheek, his moan richly rewarding. "Is there someplace we can go?"

So that's what he wanted! She'd been right all along!

"I've lost track of time," she said coolly, looking up at the sky where dark clouds were suddenly forming. "Another storm," she said, pushing him away and giving him a glazed look. She caught her mare, despite the trouble she was having walking a straight line.

"Nora!" Alec called as she pulled herself into the saddle and took off without looking back. She heard him talking to Ramp as thunder growled in the distance. She remembered Ramp was terrified of lightning. "Damn it, stand still!" Alec yelled at the horse. Lightning tore across the sky, and she looked back to see Ramp bolt, rear backward, and knock Alec to the ground. "Damnation!" He moaned. Nora sent her mare flying back to where Alec was sitting in the mud.

"What happened?"

"I fell off the cream puff," he said dryly. Concerned, and ashamed of herself, Nora dismounted and gave him a hand. "Do you think you can ride?"

"I just proved I couldn't." Seeing the hurt in his eyes, she wanted to make amends. She'd been plain mean to him.

"There's a shed where I keep sick dogs and cats sometimes." She pointed toward a stand of hardwoods swaying in the wind like dancing maidens. Lightning jagging overhead.

Alec hobbled to her mare, and she held the horse's head while he mounted, then pulled herself up in front of him. They rode along a sandy river bottom, to a stretch of granite outcroppings that led to a clearing.

Built by her grandfather some forty years before, the old shed stood under a mimosa tree, the weather-beaten sides silvery in the storm's dim light.

"I keep it locked when I'm not here," Nora explained.

"I don't want anyone getting into my medicines." She hurried to unlock the door, and Alec limped behind her. The sky was becoming more threatening by the minute.

"We can wait here until it's over," she said, going inside. Alec didn't answer, and she caught him looking at her with a painful expression.

"A storm brought us together. I guess we can take another one." His gaze caressed her face, then fastened on her lips.

"Your leg?" she asked as the first drops of rain pinged on the tin roof. "Shouldn't it be elevated?" She pulled a dusty bedspread off a cot and plumped up two pillows. "They're clean. I sleep out here when a dog or cat is really sick. Sit down."

"Nora . . ." He took her hand and brought it to his lips.

"I didn't bring you here so we could—"

"I know." He continued to study her. His eyes were irresistible, and she wasn't sure she could keep from throwing herself into his arms. The rain pinged louder, and he pulled her gently toward the cot, kissing her fingers and checking her pulse. "It's racing," he said. She couldn't deny it.

He took her in his arms and kissed her, a hard deliberate kiss that delved and foraged, his tongue finding hers though she pushed him away. Knowing she was on dangerous ground, she jumped up and opened the door a crack to gauge the strength of the storm. Rain was pouring down, filling an old oaken barrel and covering the already saturated earth. The sky was almost as dark as night.

"You're still not sure of me, are you?" Alec came up behind her and tugged her toward the cot.

"What do you want from me?" The sound of her voice was drowned out by rain pounding on the roof. He crooked a finger, and she watched his lips move.

"I'd like you to get over whatever it is that's bothering you about me." His eyes shone with what she presumed was lust. "I think we should talk about it."

"I've got to worm dogs, give shots, clean the barn."

"Later." He smiled. "When the storm's over. I'll help, don't worry." He held her hands, and suddenly she wanted to know if he was married.

"Your wife?" she asked, speaking louder so he would hear.

"I don't have one." He grinned. "I'm blissfully free and unattached. At least for now." He kissed her forehead and her eyes.

"You've been married, haven't you?"

"A long time ago, yes."

"And . . ."

"She didn't want to go tramping around the world, so she stayed in Philadelphia and I went to India."

"You're divorced?" she yelled.

"Yes!" he shouted back, as if he were glad.

She laughed, and they communicated with their eyes, his filling with brown then gold lights when lightning flashed. She told him with her eyes that she wasn't afraid of the storm as long as he was there. His brows were the thickest she'd ever seen; she was amazed at the way they flowed into each other when he smiled. She reached out to touch them, and he laughed. His face was perfect—the creased cheeks, bronzed skin, and dancing eyes. She trembled with a realization of his beauty.

"I think you're catching cold," he said, taking her hand.

She shook her head no.

"The storm! How stupid of me."

"I'm sorry, I always shake when it storms."

"Don't apologize, darling." He squeezed her hands and put his arms around her, holding her against his chest on the cot and leaning his head back against the wall. "Tomorrow's Monday, isn't it?"

"Uh-huh."

"Why don't you show me Stone Mountain in exchange for something I'll do for you?"

"I'm sorry," she said, not wanting to step into his trap. "I'm sure there are lots of women who would enjoy showing you the mountain. I've got lots to do tomorrow."

"I see." He released her and lit a cigarette.

"I don't think you do, Alec." She chose her words carefully, not wanting to hurt him, not wanting to hurt herself. "The animals here are under my care. I'm licensed to do rescue work in this county, and I take my work seriously. I don't have time to waste like other women. I have less than a month to pay off a demand note, or I'll lose this farm. I've got three weeks to raise one hundred and fifty thousand dollars, and I still don't know where I'm going to get it."

He whistled. "I knew you needed money for the shelter, but I didn't know you were in danger of losing your farm. I'm sorry."

"Now you understand why I can't just take off when I want to. I can't leave this place unless I have a darn good reason. The concert in Atlanta was the first time I'd been out in months. And I only went because of Mrs. Finch."

"You thought she'd give you the money you needed for the shelter?"

"I honestly didn't know." They were almost shouting to be heard above the storm. "Eve told me about Mrs. Finch pulling the zoo out of its financial difficulties, and I jumped at the chance to meet her. She's got millions, and I'm desperate."

"Now what are you going to do?"

"I'm going to Atlanta tomorrow to try and talk her into helping me, if she'll listen. Try to make her understand what will happen if I lose this farm and have to find homes for all my animals. If she pays the demand note I owe, I'll put the farm up as collateral. I have three hundred acres here. I can't believe she won't help me when she understands the situation."

He lifted a brow with a look in his eyes that made her wonder if he knew something she didn't. "I told you not to give up on her. She's a little strange, but most rich people are."

"I wouldn't know. I don't want this for myself, Alec.

Sure, I want to save my farm. This is where I was born, it's been in my family for generations. But what would happen to the animals? I couldn't afford to buy more property, even if I got a job. I've used every cent I own, and have nothing left. My father was from Ireland and raised me with stories of leprechauns and pots of gold at the end of rainbows. I should have known Mrs. Finch was too good to be true. I should know fairy godmothers don't exist."

"I'm not so sure." He brushed her hair away from her face and smiled into her sad green eyes. "Maybe your father was right, who knows?" He paused thoughtfully. "How many days do you have, exactly?"

"Twenty-three."

"And who holds the note?"

"Somebody I used to know. Somebody in real estate."

"Somebody?"

"Doug Dunning. He owns a lot of land around here. He knew what mine was worth and was anxious to loan me the money I needed to pay off the mortgage. That ended my monthly payments, and he said I didn't have to pay him anything until he needed the money. We were going to be married. Then that fell through. I've poured everything my parents left me into this place, Alec. Buildings cost a lot to build, and the feed bill for the animals is unbelievable. I worked for a while, but now there are too many animals to leave. And now Doug wants his money."

"This Doug person sounds like someone I'd like to meet."

"He's not worth meeting, believe me. He's within his rights, of course. I owe him the money, and I've got to pay up."

"I'll have to talk to Mrs. Finch." He regarded her with an I'll-fix-everything expression. "But you'll have to make a deal with the devil if you want me to work on her."

The shed grew abruptly quiet as the rain stopped. "The devil, meaning you?" She looked at him through her lashes.

"Still don't trust me, do you, Ms. Flynn? Don't worry, I won't claim your body in exchange for my services this time. I want you to climb Stone Mountain with me tomorrow to see the sunrise. I'll have you back in time for whatever you have to do."

Chapter 5

THE NEXT MORNING Nora was up at three o'clock, dressed and waiting on the porch by four. Her freshly washed hair was drying in a cool morning breeze that had followed a night of rain. Smelling like her best perfumed soap, her curves zipped into jeans and a lavender cotton shirt with sleeves rolled up to her elbows, she went over her schedule in her mind. She'd called the *Lovers of Animals* the night before and a volunteer had come over immediately and stayed the night: Thank goodness. The animals would be fed and cleaned as usual, and someone would be there in case of an emergency.

She wondered how she looked. She'd changed her top four, no five times, deciding an oversized shirt and jeans was the best way to dress for climbing Stone Mountain. The moccasins on her feet were the most comfortable shoes she owned, and she brought her rain slicker in case of rain.

"Meow!" Roy Bean said, jumping on the windowsill behind her and purring loudly. The cat reached out a paw and touched Nora's arm making her laugh and move back to allow the big tom to jump on her shoulder and wrap himself around her neck.

"I love you too," she said, holding the cat's soft paw and remembering how Alec had held her hand the day before. How sweet he'd been to stay and help her with the work after the storm. How much fun they'd had stuffing worm pills down Wolf's cavernous throat. She held her breath, recalling how her body had fitted against Alec's on her mare when they'd ridden together to the shed before the storm. His face was stuck in her mind like a catchy song that played over and over.

They'd cleaned kennels after that, examining each dog and cat for fleas and finding the place alive with them. What a job! She itched just thinking about all the flea and tick baths they'd given, and the billowing clouds of Malethyon dust with which they'd saturated the animals and kennels; they'd used so much of it she was sure nothing had survived but the animals.

Then they'd come back to the house to wash up and she'd pulled out a roast she'd cooked the day before. Alec had agreed to stay, if he could take a shower and wear some of her father's old clothes, since his own smelled so bad he threatened to burn them.

Wolf barked, and Roy Bean jumped off the porch. They always knew when a car was coming. She looked through the window behind her at the clock on the kitchen wall. Four-thirty. He was on time. The sleek white Jaguar XJ6 with four doors, sunroof, and Pennsylvania plates gleamed through the trees, catching the moonlight. A rich man's car, Eve had remarked at the party.

Nora watched the Jag turn the bend and purr alongside a stretch of pasture, past the half-grown hemlocks she'd dug up in the mountains and planted along the half-mile of her private road. Her heart accelerated with the car's motor, and her breath stilled in her throat as the Jag drew closer and closer. "He's only a man," she admonished herself, preparing for the sight of his face, trying to erase all signs of excitement.

The car pulled to a stop below the house, and Wolf barked once and wagged his tail, then raced to meet it, followed by Roy Bean and a harem of queen cats.

"Good morning!" Alec called, stepping onto the gravel driveway.

"Mornin'," she answered, forcibly keeping her voice steady, noticing he was holding one hand behind his back. She went slowly down the steps, trying to act as casual as possible, breathing deeply and holding back a smile. "How's your leg?"

"Much better, thanks." His perfect white teeth and pink lips formed a dazzling smile and he bent quickly to give Roy Bean a firm pat on the rump as he continued toward her. She took him in, the dark, windblown hair, the tanned face with crinkling eyes, the white slacks and pink polo shirt, the brown topsiders on his feet. His smile faded, and a deep furrow appeared between his brows. "For you," he said, bringing his hand out from behind his back and handing her a single rose. It was two shades of pink with a golden heart, still wet from the rain. "I cut it this morning from Mrs. Finch's garden."

"How sweet of you," she said appreciatively, breathing in the delicate fragrance and walking with him to the car.

"It sure is a long drive out here, but well worth it to see something so beautiful."

She gazed out at the lush green pasture bathed in moonlight, the grazing horses, and the shadowy trees. "It *is* beautiful, isn't it?"

He chuckled to himself, opening the car door and helping her in. They drove down the long sandy lane to the gate, Wolf running alongside.

"Go back, Wolf!" Nora yelled out the car's window. "Go home!" Wolf stopped obediently and gave her a sad look before turning back toward the house. "He's got a bad habit of chasing cars," she said. "It worries me."

As they turned onto the highway that would take them to Stone Mountain, Alec reached over and took her hand, holding it in his lap and giving her a long sweeping gaze, his touch increasingly familiar, increasingly exciting. "You worry about them as though they were your children."

"They are," she said seriously. "The only ones I'll ever have."

He lifted a brow with a curious look and watched the road for a long time afterward. "How are all the dogs and cats and rabbits and horses?" he asked finally. "I hope I didn't leave anyone out."

"All fine," she replied, studying his profile, the straight nose, square jawline, and hint of silver in his dark sideburns. "The flying squirrel too."

He chuckled softly, and she gave him a quick look, thinking how much she enjoyed the sound, feeling all funny inside when he squeezed her hand. She felt like a kid with him, anxious to be a part of their adventure to the mountain, her hair wild from the wind. She didn't want to be like the other women he knew, the rich and sophisticated ones. She wasn't chic or gorgeous or savvy. She would savor these precious moments with him because they would soon be spent.

"You smell good," he said, watching and looking at her smell the rose. "But then you always do."

"Even yesterday when you poured half a bag of flea powder on me?" She laughed.

"I enjoyed yesterday. I've enjoyed all the times we've been together."

She blushed and returned her eyes to the rose. "You're very kind, Dr. Knowles."

"I'm not trying to be kind, Ms. Flynn, just honest. I think it's important that you know how I feel."

"I appreciate that." She smiled sweetly but was sure he was lying, intentionally handing her a line he thought she'd swallow.

"Why don't you tell me about yourself?" he suggested.

"What do you want to know?"

"Everything," he replied, covering her hand with his. "Start at the beginning."

She didn't enjoy talking about herself with someone she thought was using her. It was true she wasn't sure of his purpose, but she felt wary. Still, it would pass the time as they drove to Stone Mountain Park, some thirty minutes away. She wanted to keep his mind occupied so he wouldn't spoil the morning by saying something she didn't want to hear. Something she believed he'd say in time.

"My parents both loved animals," she began. "They used to keep goats and chickens and ducks on the farm. Horses and dogs and cats too, of course. We always had animals around."

"Sounds like you had a happy childhood."

"I did. My parents seldom left the farm. Dad was an artist, and my mother studied to be a concert pianist."

"Where are they now?"

"Dead," she said, not looking at him.

"I'm sorry."

"My father had a small plane, and he and my mother were returning home from a concert in New York. There was an electrical storm and high winds. They hit a high tension wire, and the plane broke in half. By the time I got there, all I could see was mud and water and..."

"I'm sorry," he said again. He continued to hold her hand in a firm, warm grasp.

"It's okay. I'm over it now. It just bothers me when it storms."

"You loved them very much, didn't you?"

"Yes, I did. They were wonderful."

They arrived at Stone Mountain Park after five, driving through the main entrance and going straight to the little railroad station near the Civil War Museum on the accessible side of the mountain. A golden moon peeked from between dark clouds, revealing a light scattering of stars.

"Shall we?" Alec asked, switching off the ignition, his dark brown eyes flicked with moonlight as Nora reached for her door. "A lady is supposed to wait for a gentleman to open her door," he said with a grin, rushing around the car to help her out.

"I guess I don't think of myself as a lady," she answered trying to step out ahead of him.

"Or you don't think of me as a gentleman." He lifted a brow, and she took off in a brisk walk, hurrying across the tracks to put distance between them. "What's your hurry?" he asked, taking giant steps to keep up with her. He caught her arm and stopped her before she could step over a tree that was lying across the path, blocking the way. "You should, you know."

"What?" she asked, her face twisting into a frown.

"Think of yourself as a lady. You're very much a lady to me, Nora. All woman and totally female."

Her eyes blinked, and she didn't know what to say. He was too much, just too much. "We'd better hurry," she said, knowing that if he kept his hand on hers she'd probably faint. "It looks like it might rain again."

"Is there a shelter on top in case it does?"

"Yes." She broke away and jumped over a tree's sprawling roots, hurrying up the Indian trail that twisted up the mountain. Huge boulders piled in groups formed a natural stairway of long slabs of granite, going past twisted cedar trees and grass clinging to the rocks.

When they reached the halfway mark, Alec called to her, "How much farther?"

"Not far now," she said over her shoulder, taking long strides and moving steadily upward, higher and higher until there was nothing ahead but a solid mass of granite and a lightening sky.

The bare mass of rock mountain was awesome beneath a waning moon, the view of Atlanta breathtaking below them. They could see the lights from houses and buildings, cars and airplanes. He tried to take her hand, but she whirled around before he could and watched his brows form a deep frown.

"It's one of the largest masses of exposed granite in the world, 290 million years old," she said. "Almost six hundred acres."

"You know a lot about it."

"My parents used to bring me here every Sunday. Along with Wolf. We climbed it together. The mountain's a living thing to me. Breathing, waiting, watching us."

He laughed. "You amaze me, Nora."

"My father taught me to respect nature. Trees, flowers, woods, mountains, animals."

"Do you come here often?"

"As often as I can. I usually bring Wolf. We climb it every Easter. You'd love it, Alec. Thousands of people line the trail with torches. Kids, dogs, old people, young people. Almost everyone in Atlanta, climbing the mountain together like one big happy family. They have services up top when the sun comes up. It's quite an experience, something you'd never forget."

They were almost at the top now, walking along the irregular surface to the edge. The view of the surrounding countryside was marred by thickening clouds, but the wind kept them moving, and they could see white ribbons of road and thick masses of trees.

"From up here it looks like Atlanta is just one big forest." He came behind her and slid his arms around her waist beneath her breasts.

"An enchanted forest." She closed her eyes and imagined they were on top of the world looking down. That he was a prince who could give her anything she wanted. "Want to make a wish?" she asked.

"You know what it would be."

She laughed for no reason and turned around in his arms, enjoying the moment, the touch of his body, the warmth, the nearness. His face came down to hers, and she saw his lips trembling, thinking she imagined it until they touched hers in a kiss.

"I want to help you, Nora. Please let me." He searched her face, then kissed her again until her hair caught in

the wind and blew wildly. He held her close and kissed
her cheek and forehead, her eyes. He wrapped one arm
around her waist and they walked along the summit,
watching the clouds sail westward toward Alabama, their
shoulders brushing, their bodies warming each other.
They walked together down the marked trail to the bottom
of the mountain, Alec helping her over the rough places
and around rocks, lifting her over the fallen tree and
then keeping hold of her hand. There were no words,
only glances, until they were within sight of the railroad
station and it started raining.

"Come on," Alec said, looking up. It was dark again,
and the pouring rain rapidly soaked them. They ran to
the car, and Alec opened the door, helping her inside.
"What now?" he asked, looking at her. She listened to
the rain beat against the roof and smiled. "It's up to you,
Doctor. You were the one who wanted to see the mountain."

"I wanted to see you." He turned the key in the ignition
and pressed a button on the radio. He was a *real* man,
she thought. Handsome and virile and sexy. A vanishing
breed. As the familiar strains of Debussy filled the air,
she glanced at him. "I don't believe it," he said.

"Debussy?"

"The Afternoon of a Faun."

"Atlanta has a very good classical music station. I
called and asked them to play it. They know me."

"And how do you explain them playing it now, this
very minute?" he asked, raising a brow.

"You have to know the right people," she replied,
filled with secret pleasure. "You have to love the little
people."

"What else do you love?" he asked, chuckling in that
way of his that made her want to cuddle next to him.

"Ice cream!" she said quickly. "Candy . . . old movies
and books, mountains, woods and log cabins . . . horses,
dogs, and cats . . . pianos!"

"Do you play?"

"I wanted to do it seriously once. But I would never

have made it. I wasn't good enough."

"I'd like to hear you play sometime." He lit a cigarette and sat back like a big cat observing her, watching her pull off her wet slicker and shake the rain out of her hair.

"I sold my piano to pay a mortgage payment on the farm." She laughed. "Ironic, isn't it? All those years of lessons, and I don't even own a piano now."

"Reminds me of the story of the wife who cut her hair to buy her husband a watch fob."

"And he sold his watch to buy combs for her hair."

"Gift of the Magi, wasn't it?"

"Yes."

"I never knew anyone before who gave up something they loved for someone else."

"People give up things they love all the time."

"I gave up women when I was in Africa. Does that count?"

"I don't think so." They laughed together and then stopped, hearing nothing but the rain, staring at each other and looking into each other's eyes.

"Do you play?" she asked suddenly.

"What?"

"The piano!"

"Oh." He grinned. "Yes, a little."

"I know you like Rachmaninoff. Who else?"

"Brahms, Ravel, all the Russians. Chopin, of course."

"Me too."

They gazed at each other, something between them forming a bond, something warm and wonderful. "Do you really believe in little people?" he asked.

"I have to."

"Something's going on here, Nora Flynn. A southern girl and a northern doctor just back from Africa meeting on a stormy night in Atlanta."

"Don't tell me you think..."

"I didn't until now."

"I thought I was the only one who believed in fairies."

"Apparently not, my darling. I've never seen a leprechaun in my life, but there's more here than meets the eye." He smiled warmly and shook his head. "You don't suppose Mrs. Finch is . . ."

"Now you're making fun of me."

He grinned. "She *is* old and little, and we did meet her on a stormy night. She's a little strange too, you have to admit."

"Yes, but so are a lot of people."

He laughed.

"I do admit the idea is fascinating." Her eyes held his, and her feeling for him brimmed over, causing her to look away, almost overwhelming her. It was almost more than she could bear. If only Mrs. Finch liked her enough to want to save her farm . . . enough to want to save the animals. "I don't have much time, Alec. I'm worried."

He took her hand in his. "You're *not* going to lose the farm, Nora. You've got to believe that. Why don't we find a nice place to have a big breakfast and talk about it? I haven't had grits in years."

"Doesn't Mrs. Finch cook for you?"

"I wouldn't think of waking her before I go out in the morning, especially today. I usually eat out."

"I'll cook for you before you go back to Pennsylvania. Anything you want."

"I'm going to hold you to that."

"Okay." They drove in silence to the other side of Loganville. He would look at her once in a while, and she would sneak peeks at him, at the way his hair flicked over his forehead, the way his sideburns fanned out over his cheeks. They drove to Madison, a historic town with antebellum homes. Alec found a small restaurant beside the old courthouse with ruffled curtains in the windows and a sign out front that said: ALL THE BREAKFAST YOU CAN EAT. $2.00. They sat at a booth in the back, where they could see out the window and be alone.

"Where did you say you came from up North?" Nora asked, while they waited for their breakfast.

"A little place called Buckingham in Bucks County. About thirty miles outside Philadelphia." His eyes caressed her face and hair and settled on her lips. She tried to decide what it was about his mouth that fascinated her.

"Where did you go to school?"

"Princeton and the University of Pennsylvania."

"Brothers. Sisters?"

"One brother and two sisters."

"What do they do?"

"My brother's a doctor, and one of my sisters is married to a pediatrician. The other one's a nurse."

She listened to him talking, sitting back in the corner of her seat and thinking he was the best catch a girl could ever want. Handsome, intelligent, educated, kind, gentle, sweet, well traveled. He had the most beautiful hands she'd ever seen on a man. He caught her staring at them, and she hung her head. He lifted her chin with one finger.

"Is your whole family in medicine?" she asked.

"You might say that, I suppose." He grinned and squeezed her hand gently. "All but my mother. She's a professional grandmother."

"Do you have nieces and nephews?"

"One of each. The sister that's married to the pediatrician has one, and my brother has the other. My sister, the nurse, doesn't want kids."

"What about you?"

"I love them, but they're a long way off. I've been through that once, Nora." He shook his head. "Someone like me is better off being single. A wife and kids shouldn't be traipsing all over creation."

She saw something in his eyes she couldn't face, longing and unhappiness and a terrible uncertainty. Was it possible he'd been hurt by a woman the same way she'd been hurt by a man? No, not him. Not someone with so much going for him. Besides, men didn't have such tender feelings.

"And you, Nora, do you want kids?" He was looking at her with eyes that could read her mind, she was sure.

"I'm going to die an old maid," she said softly, hating the term. "My animals are all the family I need."

"You don't believe that," he said, leaning over the table and reading her eyes. "Not a beautiful woman like you. Young and exciting and alive!"

"Thanks, but I'm not—"

"You are, Nora," he said before she could finish. "You're all of those things. I know!"

She hung her head, blushing and pulling her hand from his, picking up the menu and glancing at it.

"I did see you, Nora, remember? In the pool house. You haven't forgotten, have you?" He took the menu from her trembling hands. "Look at me, Nora. It *did* happen."

"Where's our waitress?" she asked, looking around the room.

A woman behind the counter glanced up and smiled. "I'll be with you in a minute, honey."

Nora took a deep breath and refused to meet those eyes.

"Nora," he said, grasping her hand and holding it tight.

"Hmmm?" she replied faintly.

He grinned. "How did you get into this rescue business? The animals, I mean?"

"I've wanted to build a shelter for strays for as long as I can remember," she said, glad he'd changed the subject. "It's not an easy thing to do. So few people care."

"I care, Nora." He was kissing her fingertips and holding her hand. "I want to help. Really help."

The waitress brought their food. "Do you want anything else?" Alec asked Nora.

"No," she lied, thinking she'd like to have him. She buttered a biscuit and thought about the woman who would land him eventually. Some luscious creature who would give him children. Beautiful children, of course. Kids who would go to the best schools and do all the right things. A man like him could have any woman he wanted. But he'd said *she* was beautiful. She stared at him, unable to eat. She watched him eating his eggs and bacon and when he caught her at it, she looked away, feeling his eyes warming her, caressing her from her head to her toes.

"Is there anything you'd like?" he asked again, taking another biscuit from a napkin-lined basket and spreading creamy butter on it.

"I'm fine," she said, sticking her fork into her eggs.

"I love southern food. I guess I love everything about the South. Its scenery, its history, its climate, its women. Especially the women." He chuckled, and she felt he was trying to tell her something; that there were other women in his life. She was being warned not to get any ideas. He loved his life, and he wanted to keep it that way. The message was clear. Good, she thought. So much for their relationship. She could relax now, knowing he was unavailable. She'd remember that the next time he kissed her in that special way of his.

"There are a lot of beautiful women in Atlanta," she said.

"I've noticed." He grinned, taking up his glass of orange juice and gulping the liquid down. She hated herself for being stupid, for being vulnerable and such a damn fool. What made her think he was serious about her anyway? She'd been hurt badly by Doug, and she'd loved him. Wanted to marry him and have his kids. Never again, she'd told herself afterward. Then along had come Dr. Knowles, and she'd forgotten every promise she'd ever made herself.

As they left the restaurant, a small black and white dog knocked over a trash can and pulled out a box that had once contained fried chicken. The dog looked at Nora like a poor waif in an ad for starving children. His eyes were big, wet, and luminous. Nora turned to Alec.

"It may belong to someone," he said, taking her arm.

"It's starving, Alec. It doesn't have a home. Look at it, it's eating the paper."

"It probably has fleas," he said, frowning.

"I'm sure," she answered. "I'll hold it while you drive."

"Okay," he said.

Nora approached the dog slowly. It was frightened at first, so she got down on her knees and held out her hand. "Come on," she said in a kind voice. "Wanna come home with me?" The door of the restaurant opened, and the waitress who'd waited on them stuck her head out.

"That poor little dog comes here every day. I sure wish somebody would give him a home."

"Somebody has," Alec said. The dog laid on the ground and waited for Nora to pick it up, regarding her with frightened eyes. It was only a pup, not more than eight pounds. Nora talked continually as she picked the dog up and began walking toward the car.

"I hope it doesn't bite you," Alec said. "Aren't you afraid of getting rabies?"

Nora shook her head and climbed into the car with the dog, holding it in her lap and petting it. Alec closed her door and ran around to the other side, starting the motor and driving off.

"Well, how many mouths will this make, Ms. Flynn?" He reached over and patted her arm, smiling at her with approval.

"I stopped counting. What should we call her?"

"Dropoff seems appropriate, but I'm sure you'll come up with something that suits her personality once you get her home." The dog curled up in Nora's lap and shivered.

"She's scared. Look at her shaking. I can feel all her ribs."

"I'd be scared too if I was her age and thrown out into the world. It must make you sick, Nora."

"It does. The reward is taking them home and feeding them, watching them turn into real pets."

Sensing his eyes on her, she felt a kind of glow settle over her, something she'd never experienced before. They drove back to the farm in the pouring rain, the windshield wipers seeming to warn her she was getting in over her head. As the rain beat against the windows, she closed her eyes, thinking she'd never see him again, never feel his touch or hear his marvelous voice. She began to shake like the dog in her lap and couldn't stop. Alec was concentrating on the road. She forced herself to feel nothing for the man who sat beside her. She'd only been seeing him because of Mrs. Finch, she told herself. He wasn't any different from other men she'd known, only better educated and charming . . . handsome and rich, sweet, tender, kind, sensitive . . . She almost laughed, remembering Mrs. Finch's advice that night at Symphony Hall. She had beat the bushes and found herself a man only the man had turned into a prince and now she was scared. Terrified because she was falling in love with him.

They turned off the main highway onto the dirt road leading to her farm. Alec drove slowly because the road was muddy and full of ruts. It seemed forever before they got to her gate. As soon as she saw the sign NORA'S ARK, she put a hand on the door. "You can let me out here," she said coldly, pushing open the door and jumping out into the rain.

Alarmed, Alec stopped the car abruptly, threw on the emergency brake, and leaped out after her. "What the hell did I say to make you angry?" he demanded, grabbing her arm. He held her tightly, the stray dog between them, kissing her so hard and deep she couldn't think.

"How dare you kiss me like that!" she screamed. "I don't belong to you. You think because we made love I owe you something? Well, how does it feel to have the shoe on the other foot for a change, huh? Good-bye, Dr. Knowles. Go kiss a monkey!"

"You hardheaded little idiot!" he shouted back, pulling her to him and holding her so she couldn't open the gate.

"Let me go!" she wailed. "I don't want to be hurt again—not by you or any other man! I can't handle it." She made a fist and reached up to hit him, but he grabbed her hand and kissed her open mouth. Rain poured down on them as they stood in a river of red mud. Alec held her in his arms and refused to let her go, crushing her to his chest.

"Go ahead and scream, dammit. You're going to listen to reason if I have to keep you out here in this rain all day."

"I won't!" she denied, unable to say anything else because his mouth was on hers, kissing her hard and wild and crazy. She grew worried about the poor dog pressed between them. "Alec..."

"Shut up," he said, kissing her again and again, exciting and demanding and insistent. "Listen to me, Nora," he said finally, frowning. "We've got to talk. There's something I have to tell you about myself. I want you to understand, to trust me." The rain beat against their heads and backs, and he sheltered her in his arms, kissing her until she cuddled into his frame, wanting more.

"I'm serious about you, Nora. I never thought I'd feel this way about a woman again, but you've bewitched me." He wasn't telling her he loved her, she told herself, just that he wanted her in bed. She shifted to give the poor dog between them some air, when a large shape in the road caught her attention. Something hairy and wet that looked like a dog.

"Wolf!" she cried. "Alec, it's Wolf. Dear God, he looks like he's dead!" She broke free from Alec and ran toward Wolf.

"Wait!" he called. "Let me."

Water splashed up her legs, and she slid in the mud, falling down beside Wolf. The big briard lay still, bleeding from the mouth and front legs, so much blood that his coat was red with it.

"He's still alive," Alec said, kneeling in the mud to check the dog's heartbeat and eyes. "We've got to get him to the house and fast!" He lifted the dog and carried him in his arms through the gate to the car; the seats got soaked with rain before they could close the door. "He's lost a lot of blood," Alec said, driving through the gate.

"My vet's never in on Mondays," Nora said. "Wolf

could die before we find another one."

"Don't worry," he said, reaching over to pat her hand. She looked back at Wolf lying on the back seat and tried not to cry. "I'll do everything I can to save him, darling."

Chapter 6

ALEC LAID WOLF on the kitchen table, and Nora filled a pan with water. She was shaking so hard that she spilled some of it while Alec ran to get his physician's bag in the trunk of his car. "You're going to be okay," she told the dog, sponging blood and mud from his coat. Alec returned, and pulled out some instruments. He made a neat incision into the dog's heavy coat, and clamped off a severed artery. He took the bloodied sponge from Nora's hand and began cleaning the damaged limb.

Nora watched him, this man she felt herself falling in love with. She admitted she'd been unable to get him out of her mind, unable to concentrate on her life since he'd come into it.

"The blood just won't stop," she said.

"He's got a nasty cut on his tongue, but I think I'll leave it for now. It'll probably heal by itself." He laid down the sponge, his fast action and skilled hands impressing her, and cleaned the torn tissue and skin, cutting away hair, exposing the area and then closing it with expert care, his stitches precise and orderly. Then he was at work on the other leg. "This one's not as bad," he said.

"Do you think his legs are broken?"

"No. It's the loss of blood I'm worried about. I think he'll be okay though. He's a big dog and in excellent condition."

She looked at him across the table and wanted to tell him she was grateful. She watched him close the gaping wound on the second leg, wanting to tell him she was sorry for what she'd said, wanting to thank him for helping Wolf. She took the bloody pan of water outside and poured it on the ground, going back into the house and rinsing it out in the bathroom tub. Hurrying now, she half ran into the kitchen. Alec was shining a light into Wolf's eyes and mouth, cleaning the cut tongue and wiping away the blood.

"That should do it for now," he said finally, going to the sink to wash his hands. He was talking about torn tissue and Wolf's heartbeat, and suddenly she felt sick, her head spinning and the room beginning to swirl around her.

"We could put him in a vet hospital overnight," Alec said. "But I'm sure he'll get better care here. He should be with you now. He had a close call."

His voice sounded far away, and Nora groped for the kitchen table and lost her hold, her legs going all soft and weak like putty, folding beneath her as she sunk to the floor.

"Nora!" Alec reached her just as she touched the floor. She felt him picking her up and carrying her to the couch in the living room, kneeling beside her to check her pulse. "Nora, darling, can you hear me?"

She turned her head away, an awful blackness engulfing her.

"Nora, can you hear me?" He was looking into her eyes. She trembled, pushing his hand away.

"Alec . . ."

"You fainted, Nora. Nothing unusual. You'll be fine in a minute."

A woman with flaming red hair tied back in a chignon threw open the screen door and rushed into the kitchen. "Is Miss Flynn hurt? I saw blood on the steps."

"Wolf had an accident, and Nora fainted. They're both going to be okay."

"I wondered where that dog got to," the woman said. "How do you feel now, honey?"

Nora looked up into the smiling face of Mrs. Parnell from the *Lovers of Animals*. "What are you doing here?"

Mrs. Parnell laughed. "It's Monday, honey. I arrived last night so you could go to Stone Mountain today, remember?"

Monday! Stone Mountain! The day Alec told her his views on marriage. The day she realized she was falling in love. The day Wolf got hurt. "Wolf!"

"Sewed up and sleeping on your kitchen table," Alec said. "If you're feeling better now, I'll get back to him." She nodded, trying to pull herself up.

"Lie still for a minute or two," Mrs. Parnell said. She went into the kitchen, and Nora heard Alec explaining what had happened. Mrs. Parnell returned in a minute and sat down beside Nora. She heard Alec talking to Wolf in the kitchen, telling the dog he was going to be fine. "Looks like the vet you called is a good one," Mrs. Parnell said. "He's sure concerned about you, anyway. Found him down on his knees looking after you when I came in the house. Who is he? I've never seen him before."

"Dr. Knowles," Nora said. "He's new."

Nora sat up all night, checking on Wolf every few minutes to see if he was still breathing. The bleeding had stopped before Alec left.

A lot had happened after that. Phone calls about adopting animals, the dog feed man coming in person to ask if he was going to get any money. Then Mrs. Parnell's husband had come, wanting to know what had happened to his wife. He hadn't been able to reach her by phone; the line was always busy. Mrs. Parnell had explained the situation to him and had agreed to stay the night. Then the mail had arrived, including a letter from Doug reminding Nora she had exactly eighteen days to come up with one hundred and fifty thousand dollars.

Wolf cried once in his sleep about eight A.M., and Nora worried about him. It hurt, knowing he was injured because of her. She should have locked him in the house before she left, then none of this would have happened. Thank goodness Alec had been there. If it hadn't been for him . . .

The dogs barked, and Nora left Wolf's side to look out the window. A truck was coming up her drive. She hadn't ordered anything, and it was too soon for Doug to be taking possession. Maybe it was one of her creditors coming to claim something.

The truck pulled up beside the house, and a hulk of a man stepped down, walking directly to the porch with some papers in his hand. Nora slipped a short robe over her long nightgown and answered the door.

"Nora Flynn?"

"Yes, but I—"

"We have a piano for you, ma'am." The man gave her a big smile.

Nora pulled the front of her robe close to her neck. "A piano? You must be mistaken."

"I don't think so, ma'am. The directions here say NORA'S ARK in Loganville, and this is the only NORA'S ARK out here, ain't it? My boss got a call last night about this delivery. Had to get up mighty early to get your piano here this morning. This is it, Harry!" he yelled over his shoulder. A man stepped out of the cab and opened the back of the truck as dogs barked and Wolf howled in the kitchen.

"But I didn't order a piano," Nora said, returning to check on Wolf.

"A piano?" Mrs. Parnell asked, coming into the kitchen

with Smudge and Roy behind her.

"Please put Smudge in my bedroom, Mrs. Parnell. I had to move the kittens in there because of Wolf. And there's a new dog in my office, black and white and hungry. I've fed it this morning, but would you give it a look too, please?"

"Sure," Mrs. Parnell replied. "You go tend to your piano."

"It's not my piano," she said.

She went to the phone and dialed the piano company, but no one answered. They weren't open yet. "It's a mistake," she said, running back to the porch and yelling at the men, who were busy unloading a baby grand. "I didn't order a piano."

Who could have sent her a piano? She'd told Alec about having to sell her piano to pay a mortgage payment, but he wouldn't send her one, would he? Not after yesterday and the terrible things she'd said to him. The men came up the steps with the piano, and she held the door open for them. "A Steinway," she gasped, catching sight of the gold letters above the closed keyboard.

"Where do you want it?" the man in charge asked. Nora saw a card fastened to the music rack of the magnificent instrument. She pointed toward the living room, waiting for the men to set the piano down in front of the window so she could snatch the card. She tore open the small white envelope. "From your fairy godmother," Nora read aloud. "Enjoy!"

"Who's it from?" Mrs. Parnell asked, and laughed when she read the card Nora handed her. "Do you know who this is?"

Nora shook her head, staring at the dark mahogany piano. It gleamed with a high polish, and the light from the window made it shine like satin. The men returned from the truck and attached the legs, then the castors.

"Simply beautiful!" Mrs. Parnell said, lifting the lid. She went to get a vase of daffodils from the other side of the room, and placed it on the piano.

"It's a mistake," Nora said. "It has to be!"

"Would you like to try it out before we go, Miss Flynn?" the delivery man asked. "Our man will be out tomorrow to tune it for you."

Nora stood looking at the Steinway and thinking. Who had sent it to her? She signed the papers the delivery man held out and mumbled thank you and good-bye. Who would send her a piano?

Then she knew. It must be Alec. It had to be! But why? Maybe Mrs. Finch had sent it. Why couldn't she have sent money instead? Nora hated herself for being ungrateful. A baby grand was worth a small fortune, especially a Steinway. What was it worth? she wondered. Two thousand? More? Maybe she could sell it. No, that would be wrong. She would call Eve. Eve would know what to do.

Picking up the receiver, she dialed Eve, telling herself Alec had sent the piano. But maybe he had told Mrs. Finch about her selling her piano, and Mrs. Finch had sent the Steinway. None of it made sense!

"Hello," Eve said.

"Eve! Guess what just arrived at my house?"

"An elephant, a rhino, a zebra, more dogs?"

"Wrong, wrong, wrong. Gold Company just delivered a baby grand. A Steinway! Mahogany with a gleam you wouldn't believe."

"A piano? I don't believe it. Who from?"

"I don't know. I mean, I think it's from Alec."

"Why would he send you a piano?"

"The card's signed, 'From your fairy godmother.' Yesterday I told Alec about selling my piano to pay a mortgage payment, but—"

"You saw that hunk yesterday, and you didn't call me?"

"I won't be seeing him again, Eve. Not the way you think, anyway."

"Why?"

"Because . . ."

"What?"

Nora heard the dogs barking and looked out the window. Alec's Jaguar was parked in front of the house. "I'll call you back, Eve," she said into the phone. "The hunk is back!"

"Nora!" Eve cried.

But Nora hung up and went to the door, where she saw Alec standing in the drive, holding Roy Bean. He was dressed in a light blue suit and white shirt with no tie. A strange feeling of lightheadedness and excitement surged through her. Standing there holding the tomcat, he looked like an ad for a magazine. She knew in a minute she'd hear his voice, look into those dreamy dark eyes...

"Hi." He grinned. "I didn't see you up there." He put Roy down. "I'm sorry to bother you so early, but I came to check on my patient. I'm used to making rounds early, and since Wolf happens to live sixty miles from Atlanta, I came this morning." She stared at him. He was so handsome, he took her breath away.

"Did you happen to see a truck on your way here?" she asked, trying to keep calm.

"Yes, I had to get off the road to let him by. Don't tell me he dropped off another dog."

"No, he dropped off a baby grand. A Steinway." She observed his expression as he climbed the steps toward her.

"You bought a piano?" She tried to ignore the allure of his eyes, the cleft in his chin, and those thick, rippling brows.

"You didn't send it, did you?"

"Me?" He laughed. "Send you a piano?" He paused on the step and looked up at her, his eyes as warm as the morning sun. "I'm sorry, Nora. No, I didn't."

She suspected he was lying. "Come in," she said, turning to lead the way into the house. Mrs. Parnell stood in the kitchen beside the stove.

"Mornin', doctor."

"Good morning, Mrs. Parnell." He saw the piano through the doorway to the living room and whistled. "Wow, that *is* nice! Who sent it?"

"I was hoping you'd tell me," Nora said.

He shrugged his shoulders and opened his mouth as though suddenly remembering something. "Hey, wait a minute..."

"What?" Nora asked.

"I did mention something to Agnes about your having to sell your piano. She thought it was sad. You don't suppose..."

She studied his eyes, trying to decide if he was telling the truth. He looked innocent.

"Why couldn't you have told her I sold my tub or my van? If I don't get a decent bathtub to bathe those dogs soon... Why didn't you tell her I needed..."

Alec grinned and shrugged. "I'm sorry, Nora."

"Look at this and tell me if it sounds like Mrs. Finch." She handed him the card that had come with the piano. He laughed.

"That's Agnes all right."

"Now what do I do?" Nora asked.

"Enjoy it!" he said. "How about 'Claire de Lune' while I check out Wolf?" He raised a brow. "I have this thing for Debussy." He went into the kitchen, where Wolf was lying beside the stove on a quilt. Nora followed. "How are you, ol' boy?" he asked the dog. He got down on the floor and examined the briard's bandaged legs. Nora stood in the doorway watching him, totally confused now.

"He ate a couple of bites of sausage and eggs," she said.

"And two bites of blueberry pancakes," Mrs. Parnell added. "How about some breakfast, doctor? The grits are still warm on the stove."

"I'd love some when I get through here," he answered. Nora walked back into the living room and ran her fingers over the piano.

"Some gift, isn't it?" Mrs. Parnell said to Alec. "I wonder who sent it. How do you like your eggs, doctor?"

"Over easy," Nora heard him answer. She lifted the keyboard cover and played the first bars of "Claire de

Lune." Then she remembered what day it was.

"I almost forgot what I have to do today," she called to Mrs. Parnell. "I have to deliver the two Saints to the governor's mansion by two, and I don't have anyone to watch the place."

"I'll stay," Mrs. Parnell offered.

"That reminds me," Alex said. "Agnes wants you to come to dinner tonight. I wouldn't say no, if I were you."

Nora's heart stopped. Maybe Mrs. Finch was going to help her after all. But she had to deliver the dogs. "By the time I get through at the governor's mansion, it'll be too late."

"I told her you'd come, Nora."

"But what about Wolf? I can't leave him here unattended. It isn't fair to Mrs. Parnell."

"You go and have a good time," Mrs. Parnell said. "I'll give Wolf his medicine."

"Mrs. Parnell's right, Nora. Wolf's fine. All he needs is his pills and plenty of rest. As long as someone's here, you needn't worry."

Nora thought about Wolf and Mrs. Finch, not wanting to leave her pet dog but dying to talk to the woman who could save her farm. "What should I wear?" she asked Alec.

"Something nice, I'd say. That dress you wore to Eve's party would be perfect."

She remembered the party and making love with Alec in the white dress. "I'll dig something out of my closet," she said, turning away from his caressing gaze. She'd find something.

The dogs barked, and she went to the screen door to look outside. A truck was coming up the long driveway to the house. "Now what?" she mumbled.

The driver jumped out of the truck carrying a long box wrapped in silver paper and tied with blue ribbon. Mincemeat chased him to the door.

"Package for Miss Flynn," the man said, warily eyeing Mincemeat and the ugly pups who stood barking and growling beside her. "Sign here, please."

"I don't believe this," Nora said, signing her name and taking the box. As the delivery man left, she quickly pulled the attached card from its envelope and read: "From your fairy godmother. Dinner at eight."

"It's from her!" Nora exclaimed, turning to Alec, who was eating the last of his breakfast.

"Open it!" Mrs. Parnell said. Nora opened the box as fast as she could. Inside was a filmy white dress made of eyelet and fine silk, with hand-sewn flowers around the neckline and a deep green sash. Beneath the dress she found lacy underclothes with a designer's label and white sandals, all in her size.

"This is not happening." Nora laughed. "It's a dream."

"A fairy tale," Alec agreed, wiping his mouth with a napkin. He got up from the table and went to take Wolf's temperature.

"What do you think?" Nora asked him.

"About the piano or the clothes?" He grinned.

"About Wolf."

"Temperature's up a bit, but that's not unusual. I'm satisfied with his progress. I just wish I knew who hit him and left him to die."

"It could have been anyone," she said. "Cars drop off animals in my driveway like garbage." She pulled up a chair and sat down beside him, feeling selfish and ashamed for treating him so badly yesterday. "I was so excited about the piano I forgot my responsibility to Wolf," she said. "I can't leave him here while I go to Mrs. Finch's. It wouldn't be right."

"I'm the doctor, and I say you can leave him in Mrs. Parnell's expert care," he said. "I'd be the first to tell you if I thought the dog couldn't be left alone. Mrs. Finch is important. I thought you'd be pleased by her invitation."

"I am, oh I am!" she said. She observed his hands as she worked with the dog, his knuckles, his long fingers. Every part of him was attractive. His forearms emerging from his rolled-up sleeves, his tanned chest, neck, lips, and tempting smile. He was closing his bag and preparing to leave. She followed him onto the porch.

"I want to apologize, Alec, for yesterday." They stood on the steps. "I wasn't thinking when I said those things on the road. I'm sorry."

He looked up at her, his hand touching hers lightly, his eyes kissing her breasts where the soft robe had slipped away. "Nora . . ."

"Yes?"

"It's forgotten," he said. "Thanks for telling Mrs. Finch about the piano, Alec." She went with him down the steps to his car. "I didn't need a piano, but it's magnificent and grand, and I'm overwhelmed, to say the least." She was trying to thank him, since she still suspected he'd sent it.

"I'll tell Agnes you like it," he said, opening the trunk of his car and putting in his bag.

Another wave of guilt hit her. "I can't keep it, Alec. I don't know how to tell her, but I can't accept something so expensive from someone I hardly know. Especially when I need money so badly for the animals. I may not have a house to put a piano in next month."

His expression became deadly serious. "I can give you the money you need, Nora." He looked down at her, his expression soft and kind. "I can help you out of your financial troubles, if you'll let me."

"You're sweet," she said. She stepped back, aware that saying no to him was always difficult for her. "I can't take money from you, Alec. It's not you, it's just . . ."

"You don't trust me?"

"Taking money from a man is what got me into this mess, and now I've got to get myself out."

"I respect that. But all men aren't alike, Nora. I wouldn't offer it unless I could afford it. I've got some money saved. It's yours, if you want it. All you have to say is yes."

His goodness and generosity were new to her. She wasn't used to men like him. Doug had made her pay her own way, then lied and cheated. "I can't, Alec. Please try and understand. I'm grateful for everything you've done. You're the nicest man I've—"

He caught her hand and kissed it passionately. She let out the air in her lungs, praying he wouldn't go any further.

"I'd better get to work if I expect to make it to the governor's mansion on time," she said. "Good-bye, Alec, and thanks for everything."

"Good-bye? What's that supposed to mean? I thought we had a dinner date."

"Not until tonight," she said, backing away from him. "I have to get Mrs. Finch's address from you before you go, don't forget. I don't even know where she lives."

"One hundred and fifty thousand Fairie Lane," he said quickly. "Two blocks down from the Historical Society."

"I'll find it," she said, trying to get him to leave. But instead he kissed her hand, making every part of her body tingle.

"I know you will," he said. "I'm taking you there myself."

"Thanks, Alec, but I couldn't let you do that. Look at you, you're all dressed and I haven't even done my work yet."

Twenty-three dogs and cats had gathered around them, all wagging their tails. Mincemeat growled, and Nora knew the dog was talking to her, asking what she was going to do about this man who insisted on following her.

"So I'm dressed, so what?" Alec said.

"But you don't know what's involved. We're talking about washing two Saint Bernards, a total of three hundred pounds. They drool, in case you didn't notice. They shed too. Your car would be ruined. Thanks anyway, I really mean it, but I'll take my van and see you at Mrs. Finch's. Just write down the directions and leave them with Mrs. Parnell, okay?"

"I insist on taking you," he said, pulling her to him and kissing her on the nose. "I'll stay and help and then I'll know you'll get there tonight."

"But I have Mrs. Parnell to help."

"Now you have me too, darling." He grinned. "What's wrong, don't you want me?"

Want him? Dear God, if only he knew! "Bathing dogs is a dirty job, Alec. You'll ruin your good clothes. Don't you have something important to do? Someplace to go . . . the new job?"

"It's almost settled," he said, changing his expression. His face was serious and he looked a little worried. "I told them I'd let them know next week." He took off his jacket and laid it on the front seat of his car. Nora noticed the back seat was missing.

"Where's your seat?"

"It's being cleaned." She remembered the blood and mud on Wolf and felt responsible for ruining his seat. "Alec, I'm sorry, I completely forgot. Tell me how much the cleaning bill is, and I'll pay you as soon as I get some money."

"Don't be ridiculous, Nora," he said. "The seat's out, and the dogs can't hurt anything. Come on, let's get your work done."

"You're sure you know what you're getting yourself into?" she asked as they walked along holding hands.

"I'm sure." He laughed, lifting one black brow. "I've known for a while now."

Nicky put his head down when he saw Nora and Alec coming, and rolled onto his back, sticking his feet in the air.

"He's playing dead," Nora said. "We're going to have to carry him."

"He must weigh two hundred pounds," Alec protested.

"Almost," Nora said. "It's not as difficult as it looks. I have a trick." She pulled an old blanket from beneath her arm and laid it down on the floor of the block kennel. "Grab two legs," she said, taking Nicky's hind legs and pulling the dog onto the blanket. Alec helped.

"Is this all there is to it?"

"There's still the bath," she said, closing the blanket around the dogs's legs. They carried the blanket and Nicky to an old galvanized tub. "Hold him while I put cream in his eyes so the shampoo won't burn," Nora said. The tub was already filled partway with water, and Nora added a squirt of dog shampoo. Alec bent over and lifted Nicky into the tub.

"I'll lift him," he said. "You stand back so you won't get wet."

"Thanks." She smiled, thinking how great it was to have a man around to lift heavy dogs into tubs. She stood back and crossed her arms, watching Alec try to lift the struggling animal. "It's easier if you put his front feet in first," she said. "He thinks you're going to drown him." Alec lifted the dog with both arms wrapped around the midsection. Nicky paddled the air, straddling the tub and refusing to budge.

"Come on, boy," Alec said. "It's not as bad as it looks."

Nora pushed Nicky's feet off the rim of the tub. With a huge splash Nicky landed in the tub on his side and began trying to paw his way out, splashing water everywhere. When he realized he couldn't escape, he turned to Alec and jumped up, putting his paws on Alec's shoulders. "Turn the water on."

"You're going to get wet," Nora warned, reaching for the hose.

The sudden rush of water made the hose dance. Nicky tried to crawl up Alec's legs.

"Don't let him get away!" Nora cried.

"I've got him," Alec said. "Hurry up!"

"He doesn't want a bath." She laughed, turning the water on full force and wetting the Saint down, wetting Alec thoroughly in the process.

"You're drowning me," he protested.

"Move out of the way."

"You tell me how I'm going to hold this brute and stay out of your way?"

"Then shut up and take your bath." She laughed again,

spraying the dog and man together, then grabbed the shampoo and began soaping Nicky's back, spraying water with the other hand.

"You hold him and I'll spray," Alec said, taking the hose from her. Increasingly desperate to climb out of the tub, Nicky raked Alec's shirt so hard that it tore down the front.

"Don't let go!" Nora yelled.

"I'm trying not to!" he yelled back, hanging onto Nicky's front legs like a partner in a marathon dance contest.

"I'll just have to bathe him standing up," she said, giving the hose a yank. It came loose from the faucet and water squirted everywhere, in their faces, on the walls, on the crated cats behind Alec.

"Hey!" he exclaimed, trying to dodge the flow. Reaching for the hose, he hung onto Nicky with one hand as water shot every which way. Nicky struggled and got loose, leaping out of the tub and running away.

"Now look what you've done!" Nora wailed. "What do you want to bet he heads for the mud?"

"I'll go get him."

Alec chased the dog out into the yard. Nora watched him trail the Saint around the building into the high weeds. "Nicky, no!" Alec yelled. She heard him swearing to himself and crashing through the tall weeds. She ran after them, arriving just in time to see Nicky roll like a pig in a mud hole behind the stable. "I guess he just doesn't want to go to the governor's mansion," Alex said.

"Well, he's going if he wants to or not!" Nora said. "The TV people are going to be there, and who knows who else. We'll just have to bathe him again."

"You have to be kidding."

"Wait here, and I'll get the blanket."

"Never mind," he said, jumping feet first into the mud hole and trying to pick Nicky up.

"Alec, you're ruining your clothes! Don't pick him up, he's too heavy."

"Get the tub ready," he said, grabbing the dog around the middle like a mud wrestler. The muscle flexed in his jaw, and Nora knew he would get Nicky into the tub no matter what. She ran back to the kennel and pulled the hose off the faucet, filling the tub quickly. Alec came up behind her with Nicky overflowing his arms, his clothes and shoes covered with red mud. He ran the last few yards to the tub, puffing and red faced as he dropped the muddy dog into the tub feet first.

"He's not getting away this time!" Alex said, stepping into the tub with the dog and straddling him. "Start scrubbing!"

"With you on top of him?" Nora held her hand over the hose to give it more squirting power.

"That's right!" he said, holding the dog still by sitting on him.

"Just remember you asked for this," she said, trying not to laugh. She turned the faucet on full force and wet Alec's shirt and pants, squirting water between his legs to hit the dog. As she applied shampoo to Nicky's back and dug her hands into the thick rough coat, she could see the outline of Alec's hips and buttocks, his thighs and knees. She scrubbed away the mud and grass and touched Alec's thighs.

"Watch what you're doing," he said, grabbing her hand and holding it still.

"I'm trying to wash the dog," she teased.

"You're doing a darn good job of arousing me in the process."

"I'm sorry," she said, straight-faced. He released her hand and eyed her as she washed Nicky's neck, reaching between Alec's legs to scrub a green grass stain. When she was through scrubbing, she rinsed the dog in cool water, spraying Alec once again.

"You don't have to be so darn thorough, do you?" he demanded.

"I've got to get all the soap off," she said, spraying him again. Water ran down Alec's pants legs into the tub. "Boy, are you wet!"

"And you're going to be wetter!" he said, catching her arm and taking the hose from her. Her skin was so slippery from the soap and water that she got away easily, running down the aisle of the kennel between stacks of crates and feed bags. She heard Alec coming after her, through the tall weeds beside the kennel and running, threatening her with drowning. He came up fast behind her and grabbed her around the waist, sliding with her through wet grass and falling down with her.

"Think you're smart, huh?" he said. "Think you're the only one who knows how to give a dog a bath."

"You don't know how!" His arms locked her onto the ground. She lay on her back and looked up into his face, her breasts swelling above his hands. Their wet clothes made them seem closer, their bodies rubbing together.

"Don't know how to what?" he asked, bringing his mouth close to hers.

"Give a bath," she said. His lips smothered hers, and she felt the wet, cool grass on her back, her legs, her arms. Half a dozen dogs and cats came running to join them, wagging their tails, interested in what was going on. Roy Bean meowed and jumped on Alec's back. Mincemeat licked Nora's face.

"Have a heart," Alec said as dogs and cats began jumping on them from all sides. He rolled onto his back, dodging the kisses of six ugly pups.

"They like you," Nora teased, thinking she liked him too, thinking she liked him very much.

Chapter 7

"NOW I'M GOING to take *my* bath," Nora said, grimacing at her muddy, grass-stained shirt and pulling herself up with Alec's help.

"Need anyone to scrub your back?" His shirt was ripped down the front, and she could see blood through the wet material.

"You're bleeding!" she gasped, unbuttoning his cotton shirt to the waist and examining the deep scratches made by Nicky's claws.

"It's nothing," he said, holding her hands where they touched his chest.

"They're deep, Alec," she insisted, pulling her hands from his. She loosened his shirt from his pants. The scratches were swollen and beaded with blood, marring his perfectly tanned chest. "You poor thing," she breathed, running her fingers ever so gently over the marks. "I know it hurts." She stood on her toes and wiped the dust and grime away with the tail of his shirt.

He was grinning. "I love the shape of your lips," he said, bending down to kiss her. She stepped back, the sight of his bare chest and drenched pants too much for her. She hurried over to where she'd left Nicky. The big Saint Bernard stood shaking in his cold bath water, and

Nora laughed because he hadn't run away.

"Nora," Mrs. Parnell called from the front porch of the house. "Do you mind if I run home before you leave for Atlanta? I won't be gone more than an hour."

"Take your time," Nora shouted back.

"You mean we have the place to ourselves?" Alec came up behind her.

"We still have Myrtle to bathe. Unless, of course, you're worn out?"

"Me, worn out? Never." He grinned, bowing and waving her on. "Lead the way, ma'am." He cheerfully lifted the shaking Saint from the tub, watching her every move as she dried the dog off. Then Nora put Nicky in his crate, trying to ignore Alec, who looked like a mischievous boy contemplating what trouble he could get into next. From the medicine cabinet on the wall she pulled out a tin of horse salve.

"This stuff can heal anything," she said, digging two fingers into the yellow salve. "Open your shirt."

"My pleasure." He watched as she spread the salve over the scratches on his chest, moaning pleasantly as she smoothed the thick salve into the broken skin. Her fingers moved gently in long downward strokes, spreading, soothing, feeling the heat of his body enter hers through her fingertips.

"There," she said finally, wiping her sticky fingers in the dark forest of hair on his chest. "Better?" She had closed the tin and turned to put it back when he grabbed her from behind. "Alec, we have work to do." She removed his hands and slipped away, hurrying back to where Myrtle was crated.

Myrtle stood up in her crate and barked. "She'll be easy compared to Nicky," Nora said, leading the massive dog to the tub and turning on the water. Alec followed. She could feel his eyes on her back, warming her, exciting her. She filled the tub and bent down to lift Myrtle. Alec's hand caught hers.

"Not when I'm here," he said, lifting the giant Saint into the tub.

"Thanks." She smiled, turning her back on him and wetting Myrtle down. Alec stood at the other end of the tub and stared, moving aside when Nora accidentally sprayed water his way. "I'm sorry," she said, turning the water off and pouring shampoo on Myrtle's neck. She began scrubbing, bending over the dog and digging her hands deep into the thick long hair, giving the dog the best bath she had ever had. She saw Alec's legs moving toward her.

"Better scrub under the belly," he suggested. "Her back legs are dirty too."

"She's dirty all over," Nora said, perturbed because he was making her nervous. She poured more shampoo on, and the lather covered her hands, the bubbles floating to the roof and soapy foam inching up to her elbows. Her shirt was soaked in the front, and she could feel Alec's eyes on her breasts. Myrtle snored and leaned against Nora. "She's going to sleep!" she exclaimed, pouring water over the dog to wake her up.

"Can't say I blame her," he said, bending over to cup one of Nora's breasts in his hand from behind.

"Alec!" she said, jabbing him in the leg with her elbow and kicking him in the foot.

"I can't help myself, Nora. The sight of you bent over and wet to the skin is driving me mad."

She rolled her eyes at him and went back to work, hosing off the thick suds as he came up and kissed the back of her neck.

"Alec, please!" she exclaimed, threatening to hit him again with her elbow.

"If only I had a camera to take your picture," he said. "To capture the way your hair dangles over your shoulder and down your neck, the way your breasts press against your shirt, straining to be free." He took her arms and pulled her up, holding her against his wet body. "The way your lips tremble when you're about to be kissed." He kissed her mouth and whispered her name, caressing her face with his fingers. She gazed up at him.

"Alec."

"Yes, darling?"

"I'm scared."

"Of me?"

"No, of me."

He laughed, holding her so close that she could feel every hard inch of him, knowing he wanted her, knowing she wanted him.

"As soon as I get in the house, I'm calling my insurance man," she said.

"What for?"

"You got hurt on my property, silly. My insurance is paid up; it's about the only thing that is."

"I don't give a damn about your insurance. It's you I want." He kissed her on the cheek, and she reached for the cream rinse, knocking over an open can of tick dip instead. The quart can struck the side of the tub and splashed dip all over Myrtle's clean coat. Nora's eyes opened wide as she saw the water turn white from the medicated dip.

"What's that foul smell?" Alec asked, kissing Nora's ear.

"Oh, no," Nora moaned. "It takes a week to wear off!"

"What?" he asked, releasing her and wrinkling his nose. She plunged her arm into the water and fished out the half-empty can.

"It was almost full," she said, setting the can back on the windowsill beside the tub. She grabbed the hose and turned the water on full force, trying to rinse the dip off Myrtle's back. Alec picked up a pan and began pouring water over her.

"How do we get it off?"

"We don't," she said. "That's the beauty of tick dip. It stinks so bad the ticks can't stand it and leave the dog's body."

"I can't say I blame them," Alec said, holding his nose.

"Oh, Alec," Nora moaned, "what am I going to do?"

"Do you have any perfume?"

"No, but I've got some talcum powder." She finished hosing Myrtle off, and Alec helped the Saint from the tub. Nora dried the dog and squirted Rose of Sharon talcum powder all over her.

"That's better," Alec said, screwing up his face. "The governor won't even notice."

"Let's hope she smells better by the time we arrive," she said. "I've got to hurry." She looked at his shoes and laughed, holding her hand over her mouth and walking away.

"What's so funny?"

"Your shoes," she said, doubling over and laughing until tears rolled down her cheeks. "Look at them!"

"Yours aren't so great either," he said, pointing to her once white sneakers, now caked with mud and grass. His gaze climbed upward to her ankles and onto her legs. Her jeans were stuck to her skin, and her shirt was open. He'd been looking at her bare breasts, and she hadn't known it! Unable to fasten her blouse because it was so wet, she folded her arms across her chest.

"I'm going to the house," she announced.

"Sounds good to me."

"You can change down here," she said, pointing to an old washer she used for dog towels. "Throw your clothes in there, and I'll bring you some clean ones from the house. After I've had my bath."

"Thanks a bunch," he said, folding his arms over his chest like she'd done, and watching her walk away. Looking back, she saw him pick up a rock and throw it. Mincemeat followed her up the path to the house, the ugly pups and Roy Bean and his harem close behind. "Come with me," she told them sweetly, laughing to herself because she knew Alec was watching, thinking how funny he looked in his wet clothes. "Mrs. Parnell will feed you while I'm gone. I've got some old cheese the milkman gave me." Roy meowed, and the ugly pups ran alongside, wagging their tails. "Come on, darlings."

"What about me?" Alec called after her. "What do I get?"

"Go wash your clothes," she shouted back, chuckling as she climbed the steps to the porch. Taking a peek, she saw him standing in front of the barn, his shirt off and his drenched pants clinging to his legs. His clothes were ruined, poor man. He wouldn't have anything to wear to Atlanta.

She laughed. He'd wash his clothes and expect to dry them, but her dryer had been in the repair shop for months. She opened the screen door, and Roy and Smudge brushed past her legs, running together to say hello to Wolf.

"Easy now," she told the cats, bending down to pet Wolf's head. "Wolf isn't feeling well." The big briard looked up at her and banged his tail against the playpen where the flying squirrel lived. Chico, the squirrel, jumped on the top of his box and chattered. "Now look what you've done," Nora admonished the cats. "You woke up Chico, and he's sure to get into mischief." Wolf told her he loved her with his big brown eyes, and she picked up the flying squirrel, putting it on her shoulder. "Don't worry," she told Wolf. "I love you the most." She pressed the palm of her hand to Wolf's nose and felt relieved because it was cool. Kicking off her muddy sneaks, she headed for the bedroom. "Keep a look out," she told the squirrel, pulling the blind down on the bathroom window. "I don't trust certain people."

The bathroom was at the back of the house with two windows and a skylight. Unbuttoning her blouse, she placed Chico on a potted Norfolk pine that almost reached the skylight, then peeled off her wet clothes and kicked them aside. Chico chattered excitedly, and she turned the water on in the tub, stepped in, and slid the glass door shut.

The warm shower felt wonderful. She laughed out loud, remembering how Alec had looked straddling Nicky in the tub. She also remembered how she'd felt when she'd touched him. She shivered, reaching for the soap and rubbing it over her face and neck, soaping her arms and breasts, her thighs, reaching down to do her legs and feeling the refreshing spray of the shower.

She poured some shampoo into her hands, saturating her hair and working up a lather. Then the shower door slid open. She held her breath.

"Mrs. Parnell?" she asked anxiously. She could hear Chico chattering and opened her eyes. Alec stepped into the tub, stark naked.

"Alec!" she gasped, throwing her hands over her breasts. "Get out of here!"

"Your squirrel tried to bite me," he said, sliding the door closed. "Do you have insurance?"

"I wish he did!" she said, grabbing the washcloth and holding it low, stretching her other hand between two breasts.

"You don't mean that."

"I do too!" she said, trying not to look, on the verge of collapse because he looked so marvelous. "If Wolf wasn't sick, I'd sic him on you."

"Wolf wouldn't hurt a flea," he said, moving beside her and kissing her neck. She threw her head back into the spray of water, and Alec pulled her wet body to his, pressing her breasts against his chest, the soap on her and the salve on him the only things between them, until . . .

"He would sic you if I told him to," she said.

"He likes me." He kissed her ear and whispered, "I didn't want to stay down there by myself, darling. Not after you took everyone with you."

"You had Myrtle."

"She's not my type." He eyed her breasts. "Besides"—he grinned—"she smells awful!"

Nora giggled against his chest, and he held her close. "I missed you, Nora. I had to be with you." His lips slid down her throat to one shoulder, sinking languorously to her breasts. Her heart beat like Mincemeat's tail when the dog slept under her bed, hammering so loudly she could hear it in her ears. Tremors of desire erupted between her legs as Alec kissed each breast. Then he lifted her up, kissing her slowly yet deliberately, his tongue caressing her the way the wind caresses a leaf. He lifted her higher, sliding her upward on his thighs until she wound her legs around his back, his hands supporting her buttocks.

"Alec," she gasped as he kissed every inch of her neck and face. The fragrances of pine and honeysuckle poured through the open window, and she imagined they were surrounded by sapphire-blue water. Alec's hands held her close, and she clung to him, suspended like a gull in the wind.

"Nora, darling."

They soared together, suspended, diving, floating . . . together at last. He held her so tightly that she knew she would never fall, leaning into him for support, savoring the pleasure of his touch, the satin of his lips, the hard velvet core of his maleness. They moved together and blended into one as he called her darling and sweetheart. He was a fairytale prince, and she was the maiden in distress, never wanting him to leave, afraid to let go for fear she'd lose him. She hung on tight, unable to accept that he might not be what he seemed. His kisses were wild and feverish and frantic, and she dove with him into a sea of desire, holding on until she saw pink and blue and green, rainbows so fantastic that she cried out in joy. She knew then the wonder of flesh on flesh, each filling the other with stars and moonbeams and wondrous spasms of pleasure until she called out his name again and again . . . "Alec . . . Alec . . . Oh, Alec!"

Tears of joy filled her eyes, and she clung to him as she had that night in the pool house, holding him tightly and returning his kisses two for one. "Don't let me go," she cried, her arms wrapped around his neck and her head beside his. "Don't ever let me go."

"I don't plan to." He held her in his arms until he'd given of himself totally, whispering, "Nora, darling." He picked up the soap and began rubbing it tenderly over her breasts, caressing, kissing, smiling. He stopped to inspect their rosy tips. "Incredible," he said, lifting his dark eyebrows. She touched his face, and he bent to kiss her, teasing, tasting, sending messages of love with his eyes, turning her to watch the water run down her front over one breast, streaming down her ribs to her hip, her legs. He ran the soap under one arm and around her back, down her spine to her buttocks, between her legs. She took the soap from him.

"I can do that, thank you."

"But you do it all the time. Can't I do it just this once?" Studying his eyes, she decided they were pewter and storm and summer sunsets. She washed him too, beginning with his chest, cleansing his wounds and placing kisses where they began and ended. She toyed with the hair on his chest, the hard nipples, the tanned skin, and rippling muscles, admiring the marvelous bones and veins, the unbelievable height, breadth, and width of him. He was every inch a marvel.

"Magnificent!" she said. His chuckle gave her goosebumps. Her reward was a sweet kiss on her shoulder, as delicate and light as a bunny's ear.

"Nora, we've got to talk. There's something I've got to tell you."

"What time is it?"

"I left my watch in—"

"I've got to get dressed! It must be late!"

She'd never get to the governor's mansion if she didn't get out of the tub, away from him! "I must be out of my mind," she exclaimed, pushing open the sliding door. She grabbed a towel, picked up Chico from the top of the Norfolk pine, and hurried to the bedroom.

"Nora, you've got to listen to me." The door on the shower slid open with a bang.

"I'm going to be late, and it's your fault." As she wrapped a towel around her hair, he grabbed her hand and brought her back against him. "My God!" she said, seeing that he wanted her again.

He laughed. "Anything wrong?"

Her eyes rolled upward. "You can't want to . . . you wouldn't . . ."

He laughed again and kissed her passionately, holding her face in his hands. She mumbled into his mouth and pulled away, rushing to the closet to pull out her clothes.

"Come back!" he said. Smudge was lying on Nora's bed with a pile of freshly licked kittens, clean and damp and mewing. Roy Bean smiled over them. Male cats weren't supposed to like kittens, but Roy didn't know it.

"I know you're proud of your family," Nora told Roy. "But do you have to invite them into my bed?" Roy ran to the edge of the bed with his tail in the air and meowed at her. She slipped into her robe just as Alex caught her and lifted her off the floor.

"Move over, cats," he said, falling with Nora onto the bed. Kittens flew everywhere, landing on pillows and arms. Nora felt a fuzzy kitten struggling to be free, and Alec made a face. "Damn!"

"What?"

"It's digging its claws into me."

"It didn't mean to," she said, sitting up on his legs to see where the kitten had scratched him. "I don't see anything."

He chuckled, lying naked on his back beneath her. "Alec!" she exclaimed, clasping a hand over her mouth. She grabbed a kitten and tried to cover him with a pillow. "Do you want Mrs. Parnell to see you?"

"I don't care." He laughed.

"Well, I do!" she said, jumping off the bed. He jumped off too and caught her arm, pulling her into his embrace. His kiss was hungry and desperate. "Mrs. Parnell will be coming any minute," she warned.

"Me too." As he chuckled against her ear and fell back on the bed, she couldn't help thinking he was a tomcat just like Roy. A baby kitten clawed its way over his thigh and onto his lap. Alec's face twisted, and Nora laughed, reaching for her brush and straightening her tangled hair. Alec observed her, and she returned his look boldly. "What have you done to me?" she asked with her eyes. "Don't you know I'm falling in love with you?"

"Why don't we wash some more dogs?" Roy Bean meowed and the small black and white stray they'd rescued from the restaurant pushed open the door. "Look who's here," Alec said.

"Dropoff!" she exclaimed. "Pet her, Alec. I don't have time." She opened a drawer and pulled out some underwear for herself, pointing to a chest at the foot of the bed. "Dad's old clothes are in there," she told him. "Put some pants on so I can get on with my day."

"Your father wasn't very tall, was he?" he said, opening the chest and shaking out a pair of brown corduroy pants.

"He was too. Six feet."

"I'm six-four, darling." He went to the mirror on the bathroom door and held the pants up in front of him.

"I didn't realize you were so tall." She giggled. "I think you'll look kinda cute in short pants though."

"I can't go to the governor's mansion this way. My clothes ought to be finished washing by now. I'll get them and toss them in the dryer. Where is it?"

"I forgot to tell you it's in the shop. But if you hurry and hang your pants on the line, they'll be dry by tonight, if it doesn't rain."

"I'll wear the corduroys," he said, pulling her father's pants on. Nora plopped down on the bed, and Chico leaped off the venetian blind beside her. "That's the little devil who tried to bite me," Alec declared.

Nora laughed.

"Now what are you laughing at?"

"I can't help it, Alec. You look so funny in those short pants." She glanced at the clock on her dresser and jumped up. "I've got to get out of here, Alec! I hear Mrs. Parnell's car. Quick, run to the kitchen."

"But I need a shirt!"

"Put this on," she said, tossing him an oversized lavender blouse she'd worn to church the week before. He hurried off through the living room, coming back to throw her a kiss from the doorway.

"Get out of here!" She chuckled as he struggled into her lavender blouse. He looked down with dismay when he saw it wouldn't close.

"Nora!"

"Go!" she ordered. She heard him whistling "Dixie" in the kitchen and talking to Wolf. Chico chattered excitedly and Nora couldn't stop laughing.

"I'm back!" Mrs. Parnell called from the porch. "I hope I wasn't gone too long." She pushed the screen door open as Nora entered the kitchen.

"Not at all," she said, opening the icebox and pulling out a dish of tunafish to make Alec a sandwich. "Hungry?" she asked him, trying not to laugh. Mrs. Parnell stared at Alec for a second and laid her purse on a chair, looking again.

"Famished after all that work," he said, smiling up at Mrs. Parnell from where he sat on the floor beside Wolf. Nora caught him peeking up her robe and pulled the soft fabric more firmly around her curves, giving him a dirty look.

"Eat your sandwich and I'll get dressed," she said.

Mrs. Parnell smiled. "Looks like you two had fun while I was gone."

"Sure did," Alec agreed. "I never knew dog baths could be so much fun." He took a bite of his sandwich and made a face. "Where did you get this tuna, Nora? I never tasted anything so bad, not even in Africa."

Mrs. Parnell glanced in the icebox and screamed. "Cat food! You fed him cat food!"

Nora's eyes widened. "I thought it was tunafish." Alec's face turned a shade paler. He handed his sandwich to Wolf, who looked at it without interest, and moved away.

"It won't kill you," Nora said. Smudge came into the kitchen with one of her kittens in her mouth and carried it over to Alec, dropping it in his lap. Nora looked at Mrs. Parnell, who winked. What was she going to do? Even Smudge liked Alec.

It was one o'clock in the afternoon before they loaded

the two clean and powdered Saint Bernards into the Jaguar. Nora had draped sheets over the seats so the Saints' slobber wouldn't ruin the leather upholstery. Alec crawled behind the wheel in his short pants.

"This is going to be an experience, I just know it," he said. "We're going to have to drive with the windows open."

"It was your idea to take your car, remember?" She looked back to see if the Saints were behaving themselves. Nicky put his paw on the back of the seat and tried to stand up.

"Down!" she said sternly, waving good-bye to Mrs. Parnell, who stood on the porch laughing. "Sit down like a good dog."

"He doesn't understand English," Alec said fifteen minutes later after Nick's latest attempt to get in the front seat with them. "Do you suppose he understands Swiss?" He held one hand over his nose and spoke in German. Nicky barked back. "I can't stand the smell much longer," Alec said. "I'll sure be glad when we get to the governor's house."

Nora tried to keep Nicky from hanging out the window. Finally Nicky stood up and laid his head on Alec's shoulder. "Poor dog can't stand the smell of her either," she said. They laughed all the way to Peachtree Street. Alec's shirt was soaked with drool by the time they glimpsed the governor's mansion.

Nora hadn't been there in years. The house looked bigger and whiter and grander than she remembered. Alec drove through the iron gates with a smile on his face.

"Smile," he told Nora. "We're being photographed."

TV trucks were parked everywhere, and camera crews from every station in Atlanta were milling about.

"It's better than I'd hoped," Nora said, waving as the Jaguar pressed through the crowd, half a dozen cameras pointing at them. The governor and his lady were waiting in the shadow of the house as Alec parked the Jag.

"Who's that with her?" someone asked, pointing at Alec.

"Dunno, but I've seen him before somewhere. Maybe in the paper."

Alec stepped out of the car, and a woman laughed. "Look at his clothes!"

A smiling man who looked like a servant opened Nora's door. She stepped out.

"Nora Flynn from NORA'S ARK?"

"Yes." She smiled. The man opened the door for Nicky and Myrtle. Myrtle got out first, then Nicky. Nora attached the dogs to twin leashes. The governor and his lady came forward to meet Nora with smiles and hand-shakes as the cameras rolled and Nora made a hasty presentation. "Mr. and Mrs. Saint Bernard, your new adopted pets," she said, handing over the certificates of adoption to the governor, who backed somewhat hastily away when the wind shifted and a whiff of Myrtle hit him.

"Do you have more dogs for adoption?" one reporter asked, holding his nose.

"Yes," Nora said, looking straight into the camera. "If everyone in Atlanta adopted a dog or a cat, we wouldn't have any strays. Look at these beautiful animals. They're valuable show dogs, yet they could have ended up in a pound if it weren't for NORA'S ARK, a place set aside for unwanted animals, a haven for creatures of all kinds—dogs, cats, rabbits, horses...a home for life. Please help," she said.

A cameraman jumped back just in time as Nicky sprayed a tree. Alec rolled his eyes and stepped back into the gardenia bushes to hide. "What's that awful smell?" someone asked.

Nora shook the governor's hand on camera, and then it was all over. The cameras were loaded up, and vans and trucks moved out of the driveway, leaving only the Jaguar.

"When will this be on the air?" Nora asked a female reporter.

"Tonight's evening news," she replied. She turned to Alec, who'd come out of hiding. "Why does the female dog smell so awful?"

Alec grinned charmingly. 'It's a new doggy perfume that reacted badly with her shampoo." His eyes slid to Nora, and she knew he couldn't wait to leave.

The governor shook Nora's hand for the sixth time, and she handed over the Saints' leashes. "I'm sorry, Nora, but we can't take the dogs today," the governor said. "We're going out of town, and it wouldn't be fair to leave them here alone. Would it be possible to send them back to NORA'S ARK for a few more days?"

Alec glanced at Nora and rolled his eyes.

"Of course." She smiled graciously. "Leave them as long as you like."

What was she going to do with them at Mrs. Finch's house? she wondered.

"Don't worry about it," Alec said as he took her arm and opened the car door. "Agnes won't mind."

Mrs. Finch did love animals, Nora thought. Maybe taking the Saints to her house for dinner wouldn't be such a bad idea after all. "Get in the car," she told the dogs. Nicky sat down beside the Jag and wagged his tail.

"Get in, Nicky," Alec ordered.

"He won't get in until Myrtle does. He's a gentleman," Nora explained. Myrtle jumped in the back, and Nicky followed.

"Gentlemen don't try to wet on other gentlemen's pants," Alec said, holding the door for Nora. She laughed, and he got in beside her, his eyes telling her things she didn't believe. "Nora..."

"Yes?"

"Never mind, I'll tell you later." Nicky barked. "If you dogs are ready, we're off," he said. "With any luck, Agnes won't be home and I can take off these ridiculous clothes before she sees me. We may even have time for a little kiss."

They drove down some of the most beautiful streets of Atlanta. Nora was awed by the magnificent estates. Mansions with white pillars and spacious lawns, expensive cars, gardens and gardeners. Then the terrain changed slightly, and they went down a narrow street where the road followed a wood, turning into a long drive that twisted and curved until Nora saw a huge tudor house situated on a small rise.

"Don't tell me she lives here!" Nora exclaimed, her eyes wide as they drove to the far end of the massive house and around back to a four-car garage.

"*I* live here." Alec grinned, squeezing her hand. Nora stared up at the old mansion. "The place used to belong to the president of that soft-drink company Atlanta is known for," he said.

"Kola-Kola!" Nora exclaimed, stepping out of the car and staring. He opened the door for the dogs, then followed a brick walk through a hedge to the back door. Alec dug in his pocket for a key. "Agnes isn't much of a housekeeper, and there aren't any servants, so don't be surprised if the house isn't in order," he said. Nicky and Myrtle stood beside them wagging their tails, and Nora waited anxiously as he unlocked the huge door. "Come in." She stepped inside.

The foyer was paneled in rich dark wood, and a staircase twisted up to a balcony.

"It reminds me of an English castle," she said. Alec led the way to a sunken living room filled with antiques. "Look at that piano!"

"Do you like it?" he asked, following her across a deep Oriental carpet to the Austrian-made concert grand at the far end of the room.

"It's the best piano made, Alec."

"I believe you're right. At least that's what they said when they delivered it."

"You were here when they delivered it?" He called the dogs into the adjoining room, the library.

"Yes," he said. "It came the other day. It's got a wonderful tone. You'll have to try it later."

Nora was immediately suspicious. She'd received her piano the other day too! "Where is Mrs. Finch?" Nora asked.

"Let's see." He took her hand and led her to the kitchen, where a huge fan turned overhead. The kitchen was filled with a giant stove from France and all the right gadgets to make a cook happy. Nicky and Myrtle's nails clicked on the tile floor, and Nicky barked.

"He wants a drink," Nora said.

"Smart dog. Would you like one?" She shook her head. "Why don't you give him some water, and I'll go and see if Agnes left a note. She's great for writing things down, you know. There's bound to be one around here somewhere."

From the library he shouted that he'd found a note. "What does it say?" Nora asked, setting a pan of water down for the Saints.

"It says not to wait for her. Something came up, and she won't be back 'til late. She says we should have a good time."

"Darn!" Nora said, leaning against the sink. "I was so hoping she'd be here."

"Why don't you let the dogs outside and go upstairs and dress?" he suggested, returning with a smile. "I'll get your things from the car."

"All right."

"We can have a leisurely dinner, and I'll light a fire."

"Okay," she agreed, disappointed by Mrs. Finch, but wanting to look pretty for Alec. "Will the dogs be safe in the yard?"

"Yes. There are twenty-five acres and nothing out back except some tennis courts. Don't worry, they'll be fine." He grasped her shoulders and kissed her forehead. "Let them out and I'll show you the guest room. You can have the whole upstairs to yourself."

"And where will you be?" she asked, giving him a wary look.

"In my apartment, Ms. Flynn. I've taken the servant's quarters over the garage. If you need me, just holler."

Chapter 8

THUNDER RUMBLED OUTSIDE the huge tudor house as Nora climbed the stairs to the guest room awhile later. The dogs were inside, she'd made sure of that. They'd followed Alec into the servant's quarters over the garage, a wonderful gentleman's apartment accessible through the kitchen, with Mexican-tiled floors and antiques from Europe.

There were four bedrooms on the second floor, but Nora had only seen hers, a lovely room with colors as fragile as English teacups. Pale lavender walls, bright yellow and white bedcovers, and a chintz-covered loveseat and ottoman contrasted with the dark fireplace and even darker ceiling. She opened the box that held her dress and underclothes and lay the things out on the imposing four-poster bed. Double ruffles of creamy colored cotton and yellow taffeta hung from the canopy, making her wish she were staying the night. A bed that magnificent would undoubtedly be comfortable. She walked across the Aubusson rug to the windows and looked down on boxwood gardens and the tennis courts behind the drive, where Alec's Jaguar was parked.

Now for her bath. She turned the faucets in the pink marble tub and locked the door. There would be no repeat performance of what had happened earlier that morning. Not in Mrs. Finch's house! Nora shivered thinking about it. If she weren't careful, she'd lose her head *and* her heart.

Was Alec as wonderful as he seemed? And what did he want to talk to her about? She heard a rap on the door and went to look.

"It's me, darling. I have your clothes," he called. She opened the door and saw he was wearing a velvet robe that matched the color of his eyes.

"I was just about to take a bath."

"Need anyone to—"

"No!" She shook her head and looked up at him through her lashes. He held his hand on the door, ready to come in if she so much as blinked. "See you later." She smiled, closing the door slowly.

He pushed it open from the other side and grinned. "You're sure?"

"Sure." She laughed, closing the door with both hands and locking it.

She listened to him leave, and heard him tell the dogs, "Males have it tough in the world of women, ol' man." Nicky barked in agreement. Traitor, Nora thought, amused.

Once in the bathroom she undressed and bathed, using an envelope of milk bath from Switzerland, and drying off with a luxurious pink towel edged in lace. She couldn't believe how well the underclothes fit. Shaking out the sheer white dress, she marveled at the complete lack of wrinkles. The dress hugged her figure and felt wonderful. How could she thank Mrs. Finch for such expensive gifts? How could she talk her into giving more money to save the farm? What was the right way to approach her on the subject? The answer evaded her. She didn't want to beg, but if she had to, she would. She'd crawl if necessary. She needed the money fast, or she'd be out on the street, and all the animals with her. The dress was beautiful, and she was grateful. But clothes and a baby grand weren't what she needed now.

Nicky barked, interrupting her thoughts. She blew dry her hair, pushing it into natural waves and curls. After applying lip gloss and darkening her lashes with mascara, she appraised herself in the mirror. Mrs. Finch might not approve of makeup, and she wasn't taking any chances by wearing too much. Tonight was her last opportunity; she still hoped that Mrs. Finch would make an appearance.

Satisfied that she looked as good as she could, she tied the green sash around her waist and slipped on the high-heeled sandals. "Wish me luck," she said into the mirror, opening the door and taking a deep breath.

She descended the stairs, shaking with nervousness. The downstairs was quiet, and she wondered where Alec and the dogs were. Then she heard a long, low whistle and Nicky's bark. Alec came to the foot of the stairs and looked up at her. He was accompanied by Nicky and Myrtle, tails wagging.

"Wow!" he said. "Agnes sure knows about clothes. You look ravishing!"

"Thanks," she answered, going forward to meet him. As he took her hand, she told herself he was just a friend, someone she'd been intimate with and liked a lot. His eyes took her in, and she felt as if they were back at the farm in the shower.

"You're staring, Alec." She looked down to see if something was showing. "What are you looking at?"

"You, darling. You look like a princess." His brow lifted and he frowned, a habit she'd become accustomed to. Everything about him excited her. He was something to look at himself in a midnight blue tux, with matching cumberbund, his tucked white shirt setting off the black bow tie.

"Champagne?"

"I've never had champagne."

"You don't know what you've missed. I have a bottle cooling. It should be just right. Come on, we'll have a drink, and you can play the piano for me." He pulled her across the Oriental rug. She shivered as he opened a bottle of champagne without a hitch and poured some into a Waterford goblet.

"To your fairy godmother," he toasted, grinning broadly.

"To my fairy godmother," she repeated, smiling up at him. They sat down together on the piano bench.

"Play something romantic," he said, sipping champagne. "Something we'll remember always."

She tried to ignore the suggestion that they would be together for a long time. Setting her glass on the piano, she played "Claire de Lune," because she knew he liked it. The piece had haunted her for days; she'd awakened at night hearing it. How strange the way it came to her now. She hadn't played it in years, yet she remembered every note like magic, her fingers moving precisely over the keys. The music was sad and lonely.

"What a pity there isn't a moon," she said, lifting her hands from the keys. He drew them to his lips, kissing each finger separately and gazing into her eyes.

"We don't need one," he said. "Everything's perfect the way it is. The piece was perfect."

"Thanks." She accepted his compliment, knowing she wasn't a gifted pianist. "Why don't you play?" she asked.

He looked at her like a man in love. She dismissed the thought from her mind. He wasn't in love, not him. Not with her, not after such a short time. She wanted to believe he cared for her, that he wanted her, that he was falling in love with her the same way she was falling in love with him. But it was too much like a fairytale, too farfetched. Things didn't happen like that anymore. Not to her anyway. She sat beside him and felt herself unwinding. She'd only had a few sips of champagne, and already she was floating.

He played a nocturne by Chopin she couldn't place, and she dropped her hand on his thigh, pulling it back when she realized what she'd done. He grinned and continued playing, putting such feeling into the piece that she felt herself entering a world set aside for them. She felt irresistibly drawn to him, desiring him, longing for his arms to surround her, envelop her, hold her forever. He played with fresh appeal, deep emotion, and remarkable sensitivity. His fingers seemed part of the keys, his eyes on her instead of on the piano. She looked back at him, unable to believe this was happening to her, lost in a spell with this stranger who'd come into her life on a rainy night and captured her heart, this man she felt so much love for.

The piece ended, and he took her in his arms at last, holding her for a long while, just being close. Tears burned her eyes, and she prayed the moment would never end. Let time stand still for them so that they would never be parted.

Myrtle began snoring in the middle of the Oriental rug, and Nicky barked. The spell was broken.

"They don't like my playing," Alec said, releasing her and sitting back to look at her face.

"I loved it," she said, wiping her eyes.

"It's the champagne, darling. You're not used to it."

"Yes," she agreed. "That's what it is."

They looked into each other's eyes, and she felt herself sliding off the piano bench. He caught her arm and pulled her close. "There's something I have to tell you, Nora. Something I've been trying to say for days."

The blood drained from her face. What, for God's sake? It couldn't be that he loved her. It just couldn't be!

The doorbell rang. Myrtle snorted, and Nicky stood up and barked, a chesty *woof* that made Nora shake.

"Mrs. Finch!" she gasped.

Alec took her hand and kissed the palm. "I'll go see."

She watched him as if she were in a trance, following him across the rug to the kitchen, where the service entrance was located. A parade of men garbed in white waiter's uniforms entered in a steady stream, carrying covered dishes which they placed on a buffet table in the dining room. Myrtle growled at them from beneath a chair. Alec returned with a big grin on his face. "Dinner is served, darling."

"Oh!" she said, still unsure of what was going on as she watched the waiters march back through the hall.

"Where will you be eating, sir?" asked a waiter.

"In the dining room," Alec said. "We'll serve ourselves."

"Very good, sir." The man disappeared into the kitchen.

Alec laughed. "Agnes seems to have thought of everything. Why don't I put on some records and light the fire?"

"Sounds wonderful," she said, following him to a stereo hidden in an antique chest. He pulled albums from their jackets, placed them on an impressive looking turntable, and flashed her a smile.

Nicky barked for attention and curled up contentedly on the thick carpet. "He thinks this is his new home," Nora said. "Too bad he can't live here."

"He can," Alec said, pulling her close. His expression turned grim, and his brow ruffled. "Why don't we go outside, Nora? It's not raining yet."

"But a storm's coming, Alec."

"I guess it has to, doesn't it?"

She remembered Mrs. Finch telling her how stormy weather brought people together and made them appreciate rainbows.

"I wanted to show you the grounds, darling. What do you think? Of the place, I mean."

"It's beautiful, Alec, but awfully big for one little old lady. I don't know how she keeps it clean. I'd be worn out with the zoo and the charities, the concerts and requests for money. Cleaning this place alone would put even a young woman in her grave."

"You'd have servants," he said, grinning at her.

Now *she* was frowning! What did he mean? She knew she'd had too much to drink...

"Why doesn't *she* have servants?"

"We don't need them. I mean, *she* doesn't. Not yet anyway."

"Alec, this is kind of strange, don't you think? Mrs. Finch didn't show up for the Adoption Party, but she sent me the piano and clothes. Now, after going to all the trouble of inviting me to dinner, it appears she doesn't intend to be home."

He shrugged and looked worried again. "Are you hungry?" Nicky barked, as if to say yes, and they laughed. Alec took Nora's arm and guided her to the dining room.

The buffet was covered with old silver and fine china, trays and bowls, chafing dishes and huge tureens, sterling silver flatwear and cut glass bowls filled with roses. Alec handed Nora an exquisite china plate decorated with lilacs, and she began peeping under dish covers. There was chicken smothered in white sauce with small parsleyed potatoes, beef au jus and several vegetables, soup and hot fluffy rolls with butter, two kinds of salads and three desserts. Nicky barked, and Nora slipped him a roll. Myrtle's eyes got as big as birds' nests, and Alec tossed her a slice of beef.

"She likes you," Nora laughed.

"She likes my beef, you mean." They laughed again, and she watched him feed the dogs pieces of pink meat, laying her napkin on her lap and seating herself at one end of the long table.

"Should we start?" she asked.

"Why not?"

"I'm worried, Alec," she said suddenly. "I counted on Mrs. Finch's being here this evening. I need the money."

He put his napkin down and regarded her with an expression of utmost seriousness that made her insides roll over. "Nora, darling. Please let me help you with your money problems. I want to. I've got enough money for—"

"I don't want your money, Alec. You're very sweet to offer, but that's how I got into this mess. I'll never

take money from a man again. This is something I have
to do myself."

He pulled a pack of cigarettes from his pocket and lit
one. She realized she hadn't seen him smoke for a long
time. "You're hardheaded, you know that?" he said.

"That's the Irish in me."

He pushed aside his plate and tossed another piece of
beef to Myrtle. Nicky barked, and Nora handed him a
roll. "It's a good thing we didn't bring more dogs with
us," Alec said. He looked deep into her eyes, and she
hoped he couldn't read her mind.

"Yes," she replied. His eyes were darker now, filled
with stormy passion. But troubled. Something was bothering him. "Roy Bean loves roast beef," she said.

"You're very fond of him, aren't you, Nora?"

"Roy's special. He's my favorite cat now that Lily
Langtree's gone."

"Who's she?"

"A white cat I loved. She disappeared one day, and
I haven't seen her since. I think about her a lot. I know
she's not dead. That sounds ridiculous to you, I know,
but I think she'll come back to the farm, find her way
back somehow."

"She will," he said. She felt better somehow. He
always made her feel better, the way a doctor should.
He glanced away, then asked suddenly, "Is Roy up for
adoption?"

"No, I can't let him go. I might have once, if Mrs.
Finch had wanted him, but not now. Roy's a tomcat.
He'd be lost here with all this room and nothing to do.
At my house he's got his queens and all those dogs to
harass." She didn't tell him she was keeping Roy for
them. To share.

"I'm glad you're keeping him," he said. "I like him
too. I'd like to see him stay in the family."

She gave a false, nervous laugh. What did he mean
. . . family? Maybe he considered himself one of her doggy
friends, one of NORA'S ARK's family of helpers. She

didn't know. She couldn't figure him out, couldn't see what he was getting at.

"Come on in the living room. Let's sit by the fire, Nora."

Thunder crashed outside. Rain beat softly against the windows, and she wondered if her animals were safe.

"Do you mind if I call Mrs. Parnell?"

"Of course not, there's a phone on the desk in the library."

In the library she found the phone . . . and a letter addressed to Alec from a real estate firm in Atlanta. Was he serious about staying in the South? Serious enough to consider buying property? Mrs. Parnell said hello on the other end of the line and told Nora Wolf was fine. Everyone was fine. Eve had called several times. Then the telephone lines cracked, and Nora told Mrs. Parnell she had to hang up. She would call Eve when the storm was over.

"Is everything all right?" Alec came into the library.

"Fine. It's storming again in Loganville."

"It's storming in Atlanta too. I'm glad we're here . . . together." He was carrying a drink in his hand. "Would you like one?" She shook her head. She didn't want anything to cloud her mind. "Let's go and sit in front of the fire, okay? Can I get you anything? Roast beef, chicken, salad, dessert?" She shook her head again, and they returned to the living room, walking slowly over the magnificent old rugs to the fireplace.

"Sit down, Nora," he said with a frown, standing with his back to the fireplace and swirling his drink in his glass. "The time has come for us to talk."

"What about?" she asked, thoroughly mystified. She made herself comfortable on a wine-colored sofa and looked up at him, crossing her legs and thinking he was the most magnificent creature she'd ever picked up.

"You know I'm a physician, a surgeon." He took a long puff on his cigarette, blew smoke up to the ceiling, turned around, paced in front of her, stubbed his cigarette out in an ashtray, and lit another.

"Yes," she said. "You're a good surgeon. I know that from watching you with Wolf."

"That was nothing," he said, flicking ashes into the fireplace. She couldn't believe it; he was as nervous as Roy was when he wanted to go out. "Doctors sometimes do things, Nora. Things they don't like. Especially when they're in research."

"I'm glad you brought that up," she said, relieved the subject was out in the open. "I've been meaning to ask you your views on animal rights."

He was suddenly speechless, his eyes caressing her face. She waited, praying he wouldn't say words that would hurt her. She'd always known he might be involved in something she wouldn't approve of. But she'd fallen in love with him. He couldn't approve of animal research. Not someone so kind and sensitive, someone who loved animals the way he did. She couldn't be that wrong about anyone, could she? He wasn't like Doug. They were as different as cats and dogs. Alec couldn't hurt anything; he just couldn't. Never!

But his next words confirmed all her fears. "I'm a scientist, Nora. I believe in reducing the number of animals used in research, but such experiments are still necessary in the study of human diseases and disorders." He took a drag on his cigarette. "There, I've said it. Please don't hate me."

She was staring at him as if he'd just slapped her face. Dear God, had she heard right? Had he really said he believed in animal research? "What did you say?"

"I believe animals in research are necessary, Nora. There are certain procedures that must be tried on animals first. Surgical techniques, vaccines. There's no other way to do it."

"What about the pain for the poor animal?"

"I admit in some instances researchers aren't sufficiently supervised, and the animals suffer."

"You mean the *butchers* aren't sufficiently supervised, doctor!"

"I understand how you feel. Believe me, you have my sympathy, especially now that I know you, and we . . ."

"We?"

"I understand your side, Nora. The animal's side. Knowing you and your animals has changed me. Made me realize what's wrong with research. I'm opposed to using animals for experimental purposes when alternatives are available. I agree with you and your animal lovers, Nora. Such studies must be carried out humanely. But the fact remains that we wouldn't have miracles like the artificial heart if it weren't for animals. There's simply no way it could have been developed otherwise."

"And what good is it? Tell me, Dr. Knowles!"

"Better than anything we have," he said, lighting another cigarette. "Better than nothing for the poor person with no hope of living another day. It's new, yes, but someday it might save lives."

"Might? Maybe? You sound like those arrogant bastards at Markey's! You claim to respect animals when in reality you only respect them when it doesn't conflict with your needs. It's acceptable to you to kill hundreds of monkeys so that one human life can be saved!"

"I don't find killing monkeys acceptable," he said, downing the rest of his drink. "I've never killed anything intentionally in my life. An animal in my care receives anesthesia the same as a human. Your state puts thousands of dogs and cats to sleep every week. Mine too. Wouldn't it be better to use these dogs and cats to help find a cure for some disease that's ending children's lives? Some animals suffer, yes, but I want to change that, Nora."

"How can you say that?" she demanded, tears filling her eyes. "How can you be so unfeeling? Killing poor, helpless creatures God entrusted in our care? How could you have made me believe you loved animals?" She tightened her lips to keep from telling him how wonderful she'd thought he was, how she'd fallen in love with him and was dying inside because of it. This was what he'd been trying to tell her for days. Not that he loved her, not that he wanted them to continue their relationship on a permanent basis, not that he wanted to marry her! She shuddered at the thought that animals had died because of him, slaughtered for no reason except to help men stay alive. She bit her knuckle.

"I'm a doctor, Nora, trained to save lives, human lives. How else can young doctors learn? Computers are helping somewhat, yes, but they're no substitute, believe me."

"Why can't you use dead people like they did years ago? Not helpless animals!" She turned to hide her tears, going into the kitchen to find the Saints' leashes. She called Nicky and Myrtle, fighting back her anger and hoping Mrs. Finch wouldn't walk in just then and find her crying.

"You've got to be realistic about this, Nora," Alec said, following her. "You can't forbid scientists to use animals. Not for a long while."

"I won't be realistic, damn you!" she screamed. "You make me sick, you and all the rest of your so-called men of science. You're not a surgeon, Dr. Knowles. You're just another butcher!"

He pounded out his cigarette in the sink and grabbed her arm. "You're wrong, Nora. I think as much of animals as you do. I don't like to see anything suffer. I'm looking for answers, solutions, changes. They'll come in time. You've got to have patience."

"Patience, while poor animals die! Patience, while creatures are slaughtered in the name of science!" Tears streamed down her cheeks, and her heart felt like a stone in her chest. She loved him, God help her. She loved him no matter what he believed. She loved the enemy! "I'm going home," she said, wiping her eyes and hooking the leashes into the Saints' collars. "Tell Mrs. Finch thanks, thanks for everything."

"Nora, darling, you've got to listen to me. I haven't finished telling you what I—"

"I'm finished listening, doctor. Just remember this: If you stay in Atlanta, I'll fight you. You'll be sorry you ever heard of Nora Flynn!" She dragged the dogs out the kitchen door into the pouring rain, the thunder and lightning making her shake uncontrollably. Suddenly she realized she didn't have her van. Didn't have a way home!

"I'll drive you," Alec said, taking her arm and stopping her before she reached the driveway. The muscle in his jaw flexed, and she looked up at him through the pouring rain.

"No, thank you," she said, pulling away from him. Her dress became soaked as she walked blindly behind the dogs toward the road.

"You can't leave like this, Nora. If you won't let me drive you, at least let me call a cab. Come back in the house, please."

"No!" She broke into a fast walk. Nicky and Myrtle shook the rain from their coats and wagged their tails, enjoying the outing.

"I've been trying to tell you about my work since that night in the pool house. That's one of the reasons why I followed you to the farm the next morning. I wanted you to know everything, to understand I want to help."

"I know now," she said, running with the dogs. "It's my fault," she yelled. "I should have gotten the message that night at Eve's house. But I thought you were different."

"I'm human, Nora. I've made mistakes, and I'd like to rectify them somehow. I think I've found a way to do that now. With your help and mine, we can change things."

"My help? Me help you? You must be insane!" She whirled around and swung at him. "I hate doctors like you!"

"Don't hate me, Nora. Don't shut me out of your life. Not now, not when we've been together the way we have, not when I'm—"

She threw the leashes down and clamped her hands over her ears. A taxi coming down the road caught her eye. She waved frantically, running and yelling. "Taxi, taxi!"

The taxi took Nora to Eve's house in Stone Mountain. Eve met her at the door. "What in the world...?"

"Please don't ask, Eve, just pay the taxi. I'll explain later." Eve paid the taxi driver and Nora stood in the foyer shaking, holding the leash of a wet Saint Bernard in each hand. Eve put the dogs in the laundry room to dry. When she returned, Nora threw her arms around her.

"Tell me about it, kid," Eve said, holding Nora close and patting her back. "I was just having some champagne in front of the fireplace. Want some?"

"No," Nora wailed. They went into the kitchen and Nora sat down at the table, crying her eyes out.

"It can't be that bad, kid. Not with you dressed up like that. How did you get so soaked? Don't you ever carry an umbrella? Where've you been, huh?"

"To Mrs. Finch's house, but she wasn't there. She's never there!"

"I take it Alec was?"

"Yes," Nora wailed.

"Then why all the tears?"

"Oh, Eve, he's involved in animal research. He's a butcher!"

Eve looked over her antique gold-rimmed glasses. "I doubt that."

"He is! He told me so himself. He's used animals in experiments, and he believes in it!"

"He's a doctor, Nora. Doesn't that vindicate him?"

"I can't have anything to do with someone like that," she sobbed. "He's against everything I believe in, everything I'm fighting for. It's a nightmare!" Nora continued to cry. Eve handed her a box of tissues and made her a cup of hot tea.

"There's something else you don't know," Eve said, flipping through a stack of mail on the kitchen table. "I wouldn't show you this, but you'll see it anyway when you get home and read your mail." Nora took the *Lovers of Animals* bulletin from Eve and read it aloud through hot tears: "MARKEY'S PRIMATE CENTER HIRES FORMER

CDC EPIDEMIOLOGIST, DR. ALEC P. KNOWLES OF BUCK-
INGHAM, PENNSYLVANIA, TO BE NEW DIRECTOR." Nora
read it again. Then she cried. "That must be what he
was trying to tell me tonight," she wailed.

"He told you about Markey's?"

"No, but I think he was trying to, the dirty creep. The
next thing you know he'll be coming for Twila! Where
is she?"

"In her bed in the nursery, sound asleep."

"You don't have a nursery."

"I do now."

"Oh, Eve, what are we going to do?"

"Get you out of those wet clothes, I'd say. Look at
your dress, it's ruined. What a shame. When did you
buy it?"

Nora looked down at her dress and cried harder. "Mrs.
Finch sent it to me. Along with the piano and the underclothes and these shoes. You don't suppose she knows
about Alec, do you?"

Eve pulled a warm robe out of a closet and handed it
to Nora. "How could he tell that sweet little old lady
what he did? It would be like telling Mrs. Santa Claus
her husband worked for the Grinch!" Eve made a face
and poured herself another cup of tea. "There's something fishy about all this, Nora. Something stinks!"

"I know," Nora agreed as she stepped out of her wet
dress and into Eve's fleecy robe.

"I've been getting a lot of phone calls about you lately.
Calls from real estate people wanting to know if you
want to sell your farm. Calls from buyers at Rich's De-
partment Store wanting to know your size. Hey, that
must have been Mrs. Finch ordering those clothes!"

"Or Alec ordering them. Why are real estate people
interested in my farm all of a sudden? No one wants to
move to the boonies that bad. The farm's not for sale
anyway; not that anyone would be willing to pay much
for it."

"You're not making much sense, kid. I'm going to
the bank tomorrow to borrow the money you need. I

refuse to stand by and see you lose your home."

Nora got up and went to Eve, hugging her and beginning to cry all over again. "No, Eve. I won't let you. I won't have you going into debt for me, and that's final. There has to be another way."

"But Mrs. Finch evidently isn't going to help. Where is she anyway?"

"I don't know, but I'm going to find out." Nora dried her tears. "I think she'd help me if she knew how bad I needed—" The phone rang and Eve went to answer it.

"It's Western Union, Nora. They have a telegram for you. The operator says it's important."

Chapter 9

NORA READ THE telegram for the fifty-seventh time: TWO HUNDRED AND FIFTY THOUSAND DOLLARS IF YOU SAVE MY FRIEND'S CATS. INSTRUCTIONS FOLLOW. SIGNED, YOUR FAIRY GODMOTHER.

"I still don't believe it," she said.

"Who knows what to believe anymore, kid," Eve agreed. "It's been a week since you've received that telegram and still no instructions. How is she sending them, by dog sled?"

Nora's head pounded. "What can I do, Eve? I've tried to get in touch with her, but no one answers her phone. I'm running out of time."

"Have you heard from Alec?"

"He came to see Wolf after our fight at Mrs. Finch's house, but I wouldn't let him in."

"And since then?"

"Nothing. And good riddance." Hoping Eve believed her, not wanting her friend to see her eyes fill with tears, Nora turned away. God, she missed him. She wanted him to call. Wanted to see him. To hear his voice...

"It's okay, kid. I know how you feel. But what are you going to do? You can't find Mrs. Finch, and no one knows where she is. I've been to her house twice this week, and no one's there. I guess the hunk must have gone back up North. Hey, why don't we call Markey's and see if they know anything. He could be there."

"I don't want to know where he is, Eve. And I don't want to talk to him."

"Then I'll call, darn it. Maybe he knows how we can get in touch with Mrs. Finch." She went to the phone and dialed. Nora watched, her heart racing. "Do you know where I might reach Dr. Knowles?" Eve asked into the receiver. "Dr. Alec Knowles."

Nora waited, watching Eve's face for some sign that Alec was there, some expression that said he hadn't left Georgia.

"Thanks." Eve hung up and shrugged her shoulders.

The dogs barked, and Nora went to see who was coming. Mrs. Parnell ran up the steps to the porch with a letter in her hand.

"Nora, look what came in the mail! I just came from the post office. I drove over the speed limit to get here. Look at this!"

Nora ripped open the Special Delivery letter and read aloud: "ENCLOSED ARE DIRECTIONS YOU'VE BEEN WAITING FOR. FOLLOW THEM CAREFULLY AND BRING BACK MY FRIEND'S CATS FOR THE REWARD OF TWO HUNDRED AND FIFTY THOUSAND DOLLARS IN CASH. YOUR FAIRY GODMOTHER."

"I think I'm going to faint," Nora said dizzily.

Mrs. Parnell rushed to get a glass of water.

"With all that money you can pay off Doug and have enough left to build your shelter," Eve exclaimed.

"I don't believe it," Nora muttered, taking the glass of water and gulping it down. She wanted to believe Mrs. Finch had finally come through for her, but she couldn't help suspecting Alec had sent the telegram. But why would he? It didn't make sense.

"What a wild fairy godmother!" Eve laughed.

"The instructions say I'm to leave Wednesday morning. That's tomorrow!"

"You can't drive your old van into the mountains. That place on the map is almost in Tennessee!"

"I'll have to. The instructions say cats, plural. I don't know how many there are. Maybe fifty, maybe a hundred. I'm going, Eve, even if I have to push my van!"

"You could run into bad weather. The weather's messed up everywhere. You could run into snow."

"I'll drive slowly and take my boots. I'll be fine. You know I can take care of myself, Eve." Eve looked at her and laughed. "Don't worry," Nora assured her. "I'll leave at eight A.M. just as the instructions say, and I'll be there by noon. If everything goes right, I should be home by dark."

"Call me as soon as you get back," Eve said. "No, call me from the cat house. Reverse the charges."

"Cat House?" Mrs. Parnell looked appalled.

"What else can we call it?" Eve laughed. "It's where some cats are marooned. Nora doesn't have a name or a street number. Just a map with directions."

"I'll find it!" Nora said decisively.

"I wish I could go with you," Eve said. "But I can't. Not with an ape living at my house."

"How is Twila?"

"Eating me out of house and home. Whoever said monkeys like bananas never had one for a house guest. My ape likes everything in my refrigerator—salads, yogurt, fruit, vegetables, cheese, even my imported chocolates!"

Nora laughed. "I wish you could go with me too. But I won't be alone. I'm taking Wolf."

"Do you think that's wise?" Mrs. Parnell asked. "The poor dog's only been up and around for a few days."

"It'll do him good to get out of the house," Nora said. "Don't worry, he's happiest when he's in the van. He loves it!"

"I'd feel better if a man were going along," Eve said. "Too bad Alec's not around."

Eve's words rang in Nora's ears, and she looked out the window, across the pasture to where the horses were standing in the rain. It was getting colder and would probably be snowing in the mountains. She wished Alec was going with her too, but she couldn't tell Eve. She had trouble admitting it to herself. She imagined she felt his hand holding hers and closed her eyes, imagining his lips touching hers ever so gently, his voice whispering her name.

"I'd better pack the van," she said.

She packed cat crates, dog crates, every blasted crate she owned and could fit in the rusted old van. She left plenty of room for Wolf in the back. The instructions clearly specified that she should stop along the way to rest. She was to stop first at a roadside rest area outside Cartersville. She could stop and eat when she wanted as long as she was at that roadside rest at ten-thirty A.M. sharp. Why, she didn't know.

"Mrs. Finch certainly does things mysteriously," Eve said, yawning as they talked into the night. "This whole thing sure is strange to me." She patted Nora's arm. "I'm sorry I got you into this, kid. I mean with the hunk. As it turns out, you didn't need him after all."

Nora shook her head. "I have to give the devil his due, Eve. If it hadn't been for Alec, Mrs. Finch would never have lifted a finger to help me. I've never been able to find her, much less talk to her." Besides, she *did* need him, dammit, she thought. So very, very much.

Eve nodded. "You're right, kid. I hate to admit it, but I guess Alec is responsible for Mrs. Finch's sending the piano."

"The piano's going back, Eve. I can't keep it." Nora couldn't stand to look at the costly baby grand. She guessed she'd go through life hearing "Claire de Lune," looking for the moon and listening to the rain . . . thinking about stormy weather. How lonely life would be without Alec. How very, very empty.

It was raining hard when Nora's van pulled out of the gate the next morning and rolled beneath the sign, NORA'S ARK. Cold rain struck the windshield like needles and turned to sleet about two hours later when the van reached Cartersville. Nora stopped at the rest area indicated in the instructions and pulled the van off by itself, away from the big trucks and campers. As she checked on Wolf, she couldn't believe she'd completed the first leg of her adventure. The briard wagged his tail and looked up at his mistress with love in his eyes.

"We'll be here for a few minutes," she told the dog. "Would you like to get out and stretch your legs?" Wolf wagged his tail and whined, telling her he preferred to stay warm, reminding her of how Alec had saved the dog's life. "He's out of our lives now," she told Wolf.

She had more important things to do than moon over a man—two hundred and fifty thousand dollars worth! The answer to her prayers was waiting on some back road in the Georgia mountains. She shook with anticipation, checking her watch and returning to her seat.

A sudden knocking on the window made her jump. Wolf barked and pulled himself up to a sitting position.

"Excuse me, Mister," a man's voice said. *It was Alec!*

"What are you doing here?" she demanded, rolling down her window as far as it would go. She remembered their last words together and was suspicious all over again. "How did you know where to find me?"

"Simple." He grinned, standing in the icy rain with the collar of his raincoat turned up. His hair was wet and flicked down on his forehead like that night on Peachtree Street. She shivered just looking at him. His smile was as dazzling as the sun. "Agnes was worried about the weather and asked me to meet you here. I hope you're not disappointed."

She wasn't! "How do I know she sent you?"

"Still don't trust me, do you, Nora?" He grinned again. "This is becoming ridiculous, don't you think? Open the door and let me in. I may be the enemy, but I'm going with you, like it or not."

"I don't like it!" she lied, lifting the lock on the door opposite her. "I have a map and instructions, and I'm perfectly capable of finding my own way. What more do I need?"

"Me, darling," he said, getting in beside her and closing the door. "The radio says there's bad weather in the mountains. I'm going along just in case you need me. Don't worry, I won't bother you. Just pretend I'm not here."

She almost laughed. Pretend *he* wasn't there? How could any live female not know he was nearby? The smell of his aftershave awakened her senses. But she was wiser and warier now...

"It's foggy in here," she said, leaning over to roll down his window.

"Leave the window closed and start your motor." He checked her gas gauge, eyeing the long-sleeved lavender sweater she wore. "Is that all the clothes you brought? Where's your coat?"

"I didn't bring one. It was warm when I left Loganville. Don't worry about me, Dr. Knowles." She had trouble starting the motor and let it idle awhile, listening to the ping-ping-ping she'd heard all the way there.

"I'm not worried," he said, pulling a pack of cigarettes from inside his raincoat and lighting one. "I told Agnes you'd want to do this alone, but she insisted I come along like any gentleman would. Heaven forbid you should have a flat or be caught in a snowstorm when this antique breaks down."

Of course he was right, but she'd die before she let him know it. She was suspicious again. He had something up his sleeve, she just knew it. She didn't want him along, yet she was overjoyed to see him. It required all her willpower not to reach across the empty space between them and clasp his hand, not to jump into his lap and throw her arms around his neck, kissing him until he turned blue!

"Don't make fun of my van," she said. "It's more loyal than some people I know." She sighed deeply. "Just remember I didn't want you to come along. I want to earn the money Mrs. Finch has offered. It's important."

He held his hands over his mouth to assure her he'd keep quiet, but pain shone in his eyes. She felt herself weakening. She wouldn't look at him for the rest of the trip, she promised herself. She reached for the radio and turned the dial to her favorite station. "Claire de Lune" was playing! She almost gasped.

"Atlanta has a very good classical station, if you know the right people," Alec said. "They'll play anything you want to hear . . . any time."

Dumbfounded, Nora clamped her mouth shut and twisted the knob to another station. Alec chuckled as she drove out of the rest stop with a sudden lurch and the squeal of old tires. Alec settled back against his seat, dropping a hand on Wolf's big head.

"You still love me, don't you, ol' boy?" he asked the dog, glancing at Nora and chuckling to himself.

It was snowing by the time they reached the mountains. The sky was gray, and Nora could hardly see the road. Alec hadn't said a word in over two hours, and Nora was dying to hear his voice, ready to scream if they didn't find the cat house soon.

"You're certain you know where you're going?" he asked, lighting another cigarette. His twenty-first, by Nora's count. He crumpled the empty pack and tossed it on the floor.

"Of course I do!" she snapped back without looking at him. "I have Mrs. Finch's map, don't I?" She fumbled with the map in her lap and gave it a quick glance, making sure she was on the right road.

"If you're smart you'll stop at the first motel you see. Your defroster isn't working, and you can't see a thing."

"Motel! You'd like that, wouldn't you? I'm driving this van, and we're stopping when we get there!" She wiped her side of the windshield with a paper napkin from the fast-food place where they'd stopped awhile ago. "I didn't ask you to come, did I, Doctor?"

"No, you didn't." His brow went up and he frowned deeply, flexing the muscle in his jaw. Nora clasped the wheel and tried to keep her eyes open. She hadn't slept much the night before, thanks to him. If only he weren't so damn attractive. If only she could really hate him. If only she weren't in love with him!

"You're one of those hardheaded females who never asks for help. Isn't that right, Ms. Flynn?"

"Not from you!" she shot back. She lifted her chin and slowed down as they went around a sharp curve. The road had no guard rails. Alec tensed.

"Look, I'm sorry you don't like what I do for a living," he said when they hit a straighter section of road. "If you'd let me finish that night in Atlanta, I'd have told you I'm not the bastard you think I am. If I was that bad, don't you think I'd have turned Twila over to the Primate Center you hate so much?"

"I'm sure you would have if you could have gotten her away from Eve. Why didn't you have the guts to tell me you were going to work for Markey's? Or were you just using me for research like you use animals?"

He took a long drag on his cigarette and extinguished it in the ashtray. "I never used you, Nora. I tried to tell you about Markey's more than once, but I didn't know how. I didn't think you could handle it. I was afraid of losing you." He reached for her hand and she moved away.

"Damn you!" she muttered, nearly running off the road. "If I weren't driving this van, I'd smack you in the mouth."

"You can do that later," he said. "Right now keep your eyes on the road, please."

"There won't be any *laters,* Dr. Knowles. I'm dropping you off at the first motel I come to. You can call Mrs. Finch and tell her whatever you like. I can't stand being around you."

"That suits me fine!" He lit still another cigarette and stubbed it out almost immediately in the full ashtray. She sensed the wall of anger between them. If only she hadn't left him standing in the rain that night at Mrs. Finch's, if only he'd had the decency to tell her about Markey's in the beginning, then maybe they wouldn't be enemies now. Maybe they'd be holding hands. She laughed to herself. Silly girl!

"Hey, there's ice under this stuff, Nora. Pull over and let me drive." He tried to take the wheel, but she pushed him away.

"This van belongs to me, and I'll drive until I pass out before I'll turn it over to you!"

"That won't be long, from the look of you. You're exhausted, so slow down before you get us killed."

"Why don't you stick a cigarette up your nose!" She gave him an *I hate you!* look and roared the van up the mountain, catching sight of the sign she'd been looking for.

"Thank goodness," he muttered to himself. The van's motor sputtered, and they barely made it to the top of the hill. Nora checked her map again and pulled off the road beside a stone mailbox where a plow had recently opened a private road.

"Looks like the place," Alec said, sighing with relief. Nora followed the road deep into the woods for a mile until it gradually opened into a circular driveway. A house or cabin stood hidden by the pine trees burdened with snow and ice. The van coughed and pinged as Nora pulled to a stop and turned off the ignition.

"You and your killer hound can sleep out here if you like," Alec said. "I'm going inside." He reached over and yanked out her keys.

"Give me my keys!"

"I'll give them to you in the morning. After we've both had a good night's rest." He grabbed the overnight bag he'd brought and opened the door to get out.

"Damn you!" she cried just before he slammed the door shut so hard the van rocked. She folded her arms over her chest and watched Alec trudge up the path to the house, his black hair turning white with snow. It wouldn't be long before the van would be as cold as Siberia. Wolf put his paw in her lap and wagged his tail. "Not you too," she said. She tried to decide what to do, patting Wolf's head and ignoring her heart. She *was* tired and sleepy, and there were cats in that house that needed to be rescued. Maybe Alec would give back her keys if she was nice to him. Swallowing her pride, she told Wolf, "Okay, okay, I know you love him too."

She hopped out of the van. "Give me my keys, or I'll call the state police," she called to Alec, hurrying after him.

"This way, darling." He glanced back at her. "I can't wait to climb into bed. How about you?"

"I'm not sleeping with you!" she exclaimed, following him at a safe distance. He waited for her to catch up and took her arm, linking it with his.

"Look at that snow, Nora. Isn't it wonderful? The cabin's over there, see! You can save your cats, and I'll build a fire. I'm not going to interfere with you and your cats. I know you're here on business." He grinned and pulled her along the path. Big white flakes landed on their faces and hair. "Brings back memories." Alec chuckled, watching Wolf stop to lick the snow. "Reminds me of Pennsylvania."

"Where's the house?"

"Patience, darling. This path leads somewhere. Agnes didn't give you bad directions, did she?"

"No, but how do you know so much about it?"

"I have a map too, darling. I know it by heart."

Nora shivered, wanting his arms around her. She lifted her feet higher and higher as her boots filled with snow.

"Over there!" Alec said, pulling her along.

Nora saw it, the most beautiful hand-hewn log cabin, situated on a bank on the other side of a lake with a stone chimney, a log deck, and a curving stairway leading down to the water. Towering hemlocks, rocks, and budding rhododendrons peeked out from the snow to welcome them. "I'll just go inside and see what it looks like first," he said, running up onto the porch and opening the door. He reappeared in a moment, waving. "You can come in now, darling. Everything looks fine."

She went up the steps expecting to see cats everywhere. Alec swept one hand wide and bowed as she pushed past him. Once inside, she gasped. There were no cats anywhere. Only a stone fireplace and open beams, calico wallpaper and rough, handmade furniture, country coziness and charm.

"Like it?"

"Where are the cats?"

"Let's see." He took her hand, and they went into the bedroom. "They must be around here somewhere." Nora examined every inch of the place. The bedroom contained a wide bed made of skinned pine posts and was covered with patchwork quilts just begging to be laid on. Nora heard mewing and stopped to listen. Alec paused too.

"Kittens!" she exclaimed.

"I believe you're right," he agreed. They hurried into the adjoining bathroom. The white bathtub was filled with kittens, dark and tiger-striped and very young.

"Five of them!"

"Six," Alec said, pulling one out from behind the commode. "Six little kittens who've lost their mittens, all waiting to be saved." He chuckled.

"Where's their mother?"

Alec shrugged. "Look around. I'm going to get in some wood before it's too dark to see." While he was gone, she searched the cabin for more cats. She found an atrium dining room and kitchen linked to the rest of the house by a long sun deck. Nora wondered who the cabin belonged to and marveled at the use of natural materials and expert craftmanship.

"Like it?" Alec asked as he carried in a load of logs and set them down in front of the fireplace.

"I don't see any more cats," she said, disappointed because she'd expected to find dozens. She wanted to earn the money, not to steal it.

The baby kittens mewed and scratched to get out of the tub. Nora decided they were hungry and went to the kitchen with Wolf to look for food. She discovered a full pantry stocked as if in preparation for a blizzard; she opened a can of milk, suspecting Alec of setting her up but deciding to play along.

"Don't you think it's romantic?" he asked when she returned to the living room. The curtains were billowing from a draft, and snow stung the windows.

"It's colder in here than outside,"she said, rubbing her hands and arms. "Do we have plenty of wood?"

"Plenty, darling. I'll have the place warmed up before you can get undressed. Why don't you go into the bedroom and get comfortable? Take off your clothes and unwind." He gave her his best grin, with dimples that turned her into cooked spaghetti.

"I'll bring in some wood," she said, heading for the outside deck. He caught her arm before she could reach the door.

"I came along to take care of you, Nora. I know you'll never admit it, but you need a man."

"The only thing I *need* is money, Doctor. I know how to bring in wood and I can build a fire too." She pushed his hand away.

"I know you're tired, darling. Why don't you go to bed? I'll take care of the fire and join you soon."

She wasn't going to bed at all, if she could help it. She went back to the bathroom to check on the kittens. Their bellies were full, and they were licking their paws. Nora emptied a basket of magazines in the bedroom, loaded it up with kittens, and returned to watch Alec build the fire. She sat on a calico-covered window seat at the bay window and filled her eyes with his broad back and narrow waist as he stretched and twisted. She noticed the way his hair turned up where it touched the collar of his shirt, the way his ears turned pink when the fire started. She didn't know doctors could build fires. She didn't really know much of anything about him, except that he did work she detested. He got the fire going quickly and stood looking at her, the blaze behind him.

"What are you staring at?" she asked.

"Your face in the firelight. It's lovely."

"So is yours." She pulled her feet under her and dragged the basket of kittens closer to the fire. She'd probably sleep on the window seat. She certainly wasn't sleeping with him!

"You don't know how to accept a compliment, do you?"

"Not from you," she said softly, watching him standing there with his legs apart, the silver buckle on his belt gleaming in the firelight.

"Why the hell not? Because you think I'm a butcher, or because you're afraid to be a woman?"

She looked up at him, ready to talk, to fight if necessary. "Suppose I am afraid? Suppose I've given up being a woman? Why shouldn't I be afraid? Everytime I'm a woman I get used, or hurt, or both."

"Don't be afraid, Nora." His face was half in shadow, his brow creasing in concern. "I won't hurt you, I promise."

"You've already hurt me," she said, trying not to cry. "You've used me the way men always use women. You got me in bed knowing I'd hate you in the end."

"That's not true." He came closer. "What happened in the pool house was beyond both of us. There was magic between us that night, and you know it. Sure, I knew you wouldn't approve if you knew what I did for a living. But what was I to you? We'd only met, and you didn't like me. Not even after we'd made love. You left, remember? I followed you to the farm that morning because I wanted to see you again. Sex was part of it, yes, but mostly it was you, Nora. I wanted you! Do you understand? I never wanted us to end."

Her hands were shaking. She wanted to believe him. But she couldn't.

"I don't believe you. You're like all the rest. You

knew how I felt about animal rights, yet you said nothing. What were you waiting for?"

"You'd lost your faith in men, darling. I don't blame you, but I wanted to get you over that first. Everytime I tried to tell you what I did, something prevented it. All doctors are in research at one time or another. I'm the kind of doctor who's searching for cures. I accepted the job with the Primate Center because I knew they needed someone who cared about the apes. Don't you see what it means, darling? I can be on the inside where it's happening, where I can help!"

"No, I don't see. I don't see how you could set foot in that horrible place. It's nothing but a torture chamber for apes. Everyone knows that. Do you think I'm stupid?"

"I think you're very intelligent, Nora. But you've let passion get in the way of logic. As director of Markey's I can make certain every test is done with the animal's welfare in mind. I'll make damn sure the apes are treated humanely."

"But I don't want the apes there, Alec. You just don't understand, do you? The animals are oppressed and need liberating. I don't care about improved conditions for them, but about their *rights*, the right not to be experimented on!" She fell back against the pillows and felt the cold air of the snowstorm on her neck.

"If I took you in my arms, would you understand?"

"Don't touch me, Alec. I have to think. Leave me alone, please."

"Okay, I will." He walked over to her and reached out his hand, then pulled it back. "It's still coming down out there." He rubbed his hand on his leg, walked back to the fireplace, and leaned against the stone mantel, gazing into the flames. "We'll be snowed in by morning."

Snowed in! Her back stiffened. Stranded in a cabin in the mountains with this hunk! God help her, what would she do?

She heard Alec go into the bathroom and close the door. She'd have to spend the night in a chair in front of the fire, that's all. She could hear water running in the bathroom while she looked under the window seat for blankets. Then the commode flushed, and she ran back to the window seat, sitting very still beside the basket of sleeping kittens.

"Good night," Alec said, opening and closing the bedroom door.

"Night," she whispered, staring at the reflection of dancing flames on the pine ceiling. She smelled burning wood and sighed. What did Alec look like in his pajamas? What had he meant about her needing a man? His remark about her face in the firelight had nearly made her jump into his arms!

The fire cracked and snapped, and she closed her eyes, wanting nothing more than his arms around her. If only she could sleep a couple of hours and then somehow get the van keys, she could sneak out and leave him behind. She settled into the rocker next to the fireplace and tried to forget Dr. Alec Knowles. Tomorrow she would receive the money for rescuing the cats, the money that would save her farm and build NORA'S ARK.

Several hours later Nora opened her eyes. Could she have slept? She glanced at her watch and couldn't believe the time. The wind howled outside, sounding like it might blow off the cabin roof, and the dying fire sputtered.

Something had awakened her. A tree scratching against the house? A mouse? A rat? If there was a rat around, she'd die. She sat up in the rocker and stared at the bedroom door. How could Alec sleep when it was so cold? Her nose felt like an ice cube, and her feet were numb.

"Alec," she whispered, half afraid he'd wake up and hoping desperately he would. "Alec!" She rubbed her stiff fingers together, craning her neck to see Wolf. The big briard continued to sleep peacefully. "Wolf. Wolf." The dog let out a snort and wagged his tail, rolling over and going back to sleep. "Some guard dog you are!" she muttered.

She went across the room to where Alec had left his boots by the door. Hers were short and soaked, but his were tall, lined with fur, and felt good when she slipped her bare feet inside. She'd have to go out on the deck to get wood, and she didn't want to walk barefoot in the snow.

Opening the door slowly, she tried not to make a sound. The deck was covered with at least two inches of new snow, which continued to fall heavily. She held onto the railing and eased herself across to the steps, looking for firewood. There wasn't any.

Something made a shuffling sound behind her. "Wolf?" she whispered, remembering she'd left the door ajar. Turning slowly, she glanced over her shoulder at something big and hairy that shook snow off its coat. It was dark, and she couldn't see clearly. Whatever it was stood up and waved a paw. "Wolf?" The shape let out a low, ominous growl. She screamed—*"Alec!"*—and fell sideway down the steps, catching her foot between them. At the bottom she lay very still and waited to be devoured. Nothing moved. Then the door of the cabin burst open with a bang, and Alec stood there, poised for action. Wolf's head appeared between his legs. The dog growled, then ran yelping into the cabin.

"Nora?" Alec called, peering out onto the snow-covered deck.

"Here." Nora moaned. "On the steps."

"Nora!" Alec rushed forward and hurried down the steps in his bare feet. He loosened her foot from between the steps and helped her up. "Are you all right?"

"Bearrr!" she whispered, knowing the bear was still on the deck behind him.

"You poor darling, you're freezing." He brushed the snow from her face.

"Bearr."

"I know you're cold, darling. I'll get you warmed up as soon as we get inside." He slid his arm around her back and lifted her into his arms, carrying her up the steps as Wolf howled inside the cabin.

"Bearrr!" she screamed as a huge brown bear stood up out of the shadows and came down the steps toward them. She threw her arms around Alec's neck and felt him falling backward. The bear jumped over the railing, landed on all fours, and ran off while Alec and Nora fell backward into a snowdrift.

"That was a bear!" Alec shouted, holding Nora close and kissing her cheek. He laughed and looked up into the sky. "Imagine, snow in Georgia and me holding a southern lady."

"Let me up!"

"Hold still, hardhead," he said, pressing her close. Her face was caked in snow, and she shivered in his arms. He brushed the flakes from her cheeks, kissing some from her nose, her mouth. She closed her eyes and felt the warm flow of desire heating her limbs. Alec turned her into his embrace, cradling her to him for a long moment. "What were you doing? Trying to rescue the bear?" he asked.

"We . . . were . . . out . . . of . . . wood." She shivered, her teeth chattering. He brushed the snow from her jeans and sweater and helped her to her feet, then picked her up in his arms again.

"Shall we try again?" He chuckled, climbing the steps cautiously, crossing the deck and kicking open the door with his foot. Wolf barked and stood with his tail between his legs. "It's only us," Alec said. "Your dog's a coward," he told Nora as he carried her to the bedroom. "Now, to get your clothes off."

"Noo . . ."

"Yes, young lady. I know you don't like being told what to do, and I accept that, but this is an exception. There's a bear outside, and you're staying put for the night if I have to sit on you."

"No, Alec!"

His reply was a deep kiss that made her see double, his tongue touching hers as he laid her gently on the quilted bed.

"Damn!" she muttered, knowing she was done for.

"Go ahead and swear if it makes you happy. You're so wrapped up with the needs of animals that you've forgotten how it feels to be a woman. You're female, my darling. A woman who needs a man. Admit it to yourself. Admit it to me."

"I won't!"

He kissed her open mouth as if he were giving mouth-to-mouth resuscitation, his lips engulfing hers, begging them to open. She held her mouth shut and pressed her hands into the soft hair on his chest beneath his pajamas. He kissed her forehead and pulled the pins from the knot of hair at the back of her head, releasing a mass of wet curls that bloomed like magnolia blossoms over the pillow.

"You're a woman, Nora. Warm and delicious and designed for loving, designed for a man."

She tried to protest, but couldn't. He kissed her again, gently rolling over her on the bed. She trembled and searched his face for answers. Could he possibly love her, Nora Flynn, the crazy lady from Walton County who collected strays and had forgotten how it felt to be a woman? He couldn't love her. Not the handsome northerner who looked more like a prince than a doctor. Not the hunk who could get any woman he wanted. She was plain and poor and, right now, about as sexy as a wet bunny. Alec's eyes flashed in the dark, and a storm raged in her head, threatening to blow her away. She hated what he did for a living, but it didn't seem to matter so much now. She loved him with all her heart.

"I won't force you," he said, admiring her as he sat back and lifted his brow. "I want to kiss every precious inch of you, but you have to want me to do it." He kissed her lips sweetly, pressing himself to her, caressing her face and eyes and neck, undoing the buttons on the shoulder of her sweater and running his fingertips along the base of her neck. He kissed her collarbone and looked down at her. "You're the woman I want, Nora. Hot tempered, yes, but also softhearted and filled with love. You're in my head, and I can't get you out."

He nibbled her ear, and his lips caressed her hairline, nuzzling closer and closer until his breath tickled her ear and she closed her eyes. "I went back to Pennsylvania to try and forget you, but I couldn't. I want you, Nora. I want you now." He ran the tip of his tongue down the ridge of her jaw to her mouth, kissing her passionately, hungrily, faster and faster, more kisses than she could count, his tongue touching hers, inviting hers, tempting her more and more until she kissed him back, his eyes, nose, cheeks, and lips. "Nora, darling," he whispered, holding her in his arms.

"Darling," she said back, wrapping herself around him and holding tight.

"I've thought of nothing but you since that night in Atlanta. I can still see you in that white dress with the Saints at your feet, playing the piano for me and just being with me. How wonderful it was to spend that time with you, Nora. I was going to go up North today, but I just couldn't. Not without seeing you again, not without explaining." He kissed her mouth. "I went to a lot of trouble to follow you to Cartersville. Do you think I'd go out in a snowstorm with a woman in an old van if she didn't mean something to me?" He unbuttoned his belt and undid his jeans, smiling down at her as he slid them off.

"What are you doing?"

"Getting in bed with you before you freeze."

"No, Alec, please. That's not fair. I can't be responsible for what might happen."

"I'll be responsible," he said. "Do you want to be sick? Then who would take care of your animals? I'm going to make love to you, Nora. Sweet, old-fashioned love." He pulled off the boot she still wore, unzipped her jeans, and peeled them slowly down her legs. Next came her lavender sweater, already unbuttoned and hanging off one shoulder. She was naked except for her underpants. Alec moaned, lying on one shoulder to look at her. She covered her breasts with her hands, but he removed them gently, kissing her fingers and then holding her hands while he kissed her breasts. She shivered, and he pulled the quilt up to cover her.

"Better?"

"Hmmm." She nodded. The storm that had raged between them was only a distant rumble now. She'd surrendered to the enemy and now lay in his arms like a budding flower, sunning herself in the warm current of emotion that flowed between them, losing her hurt and anger to his kisses, becoming a woman again.

Chapter 10

NORA STIRRED BENEATH the patchwork quilt, a smile on her face as she smelled bacon cooking, sweet wood smoke, and the fragrance of flowers. She opened her eyes and saw Alec sitting on the window seat watching her.

"Alec, why didn't you wake me? What time is it?"

"It's early. The sun's just coming up. Wrap the quilt around you and come out on the deck with me. I want to show you something." He came over to the bed and kissed her, then took her hands and pulled her up.

"I can't believe this place has only one quilt," she said. "We would have frozen to death last night if we hadn't . . ." She stopped, looking up at him and smiling, holding the quilt to her breasts.

"Slept together?" he finished, pulling her into his embrace as they walked to the door.

A cold draft of mountain air made her gasp, as did the sight that met her eyes.

A thick layer of virgin snow covered everything but the lake, looking like powdered sugar. The trees were

coated with ice that dripped like frosting onto the rhododendrons, which were still heavy with lavender blooms.
The sun coming up on the other side of the mountain
behind the lake made the snow glisten like diamonds,
turning it pink, purple, and gold.

"It's so utterly beautiful, Alec. I'm afraid I might cry."

"Don't cry, darling. Remember this moment. It snowed
for us, so that we'd be together."

She looked up into his eyes and hoped hers wouldn't
give her away. She didn't want him to know how much
she loved him—more than her farm, more than her animals, more than her principles. He looked down at her,
this tall doctor she'd hated only hours before, and felt
happy to be a woman, thrilled to be alive, content to be
with him.

"Look!" he said softly. "A deer on the other side of
the lake. A buck with quite a rack of antlers. Wait here,
and I'll go get my binoculars." She watched the deer,
then turned to see Alec get down a pair of binoculars
from behind some books in one of the bookcases that
flanked the living room fireplace. She went inside to
warm herself in front of the fire.

"We don't have time to look at wildlife, Alec. I'm
sorry, but I've got to get back. Where are my clothes?"

"You look great in a quilt," he said. "Come on, I
cooked breakfast, and you're going to have it in bed."

"I've never had breakfast in bed in my life," she
protested.

"Then it's high time you did, Ms. Flynn."

"Alec," she said as he took her hand and pulled her
into the bedroom. "I have to get dressed. I came here to
save some cats." She studied his face. "The cats I found
last night were anything but starved, Doctor."

"I know," he said in a guilty tone. "Come into the
kitchen, and we'll talk. We're snowed in for a while yet,
until it melts."

"Who's house is this, Alec? Do you know?" Guiding
her to the kitchen by way of the glassed-in deck, he
didn't answer.

"Sit down, Nora." He seated her at a long table in front of a big window overlooking the lake. A bowl of lilacs on the table reminded her of their night together in the pool house, the first time they'd made love.

"Where did the lilacs come from?" she asked.

He went to the big black stove and brought her a plate of scrambled eggs and bacon with a buttered English muffin, and sat down beside her, looking like Roy Bean after a bad night with the toms.

"I had them sent up yesterday."

"Yesterday?" She laughed, thinking he was joking. "We didn't arrive until last night, Doctor."

"Aren't you eating?" he asked.

"I'm not hungry. What's going on here, Alec? How did you know where to find those binoculars? Who owns this cabin?"

He went back to the stove and lit a cigarette. After last night she'd almost forgotten their differences, but now they were returning with a vengeance.

"The man who takes care of this cabin called me a couple of days ago and said my cat got run over by a car. Last Christmas a stray took up residence under the deck. My dad was here at the time and told me about the cat. Then the kittens arrived . . . the ones you found last night."

"Do you own the cabin?"

"Yes, but I haven't been here in years. I built it when I thought I'd be based in Atlanta." He took a long draw on his cigarette. "I told Mrs. Finch about the kittens, and she wanted to help. She wanted to help you too. She decided to offer you the money you needed in return for saving the kittens. She knew things weren't going well between us after that night in Atlanta, and she wanted to get us back together again. She asked me to meet you at Cartersville. Of course I was glad to oblige. Agnes thought if we got away by ourselves . . . away from the dogs and cats and monkeys, friends, work, your farm . . ."

Thoughts raced through Nora's mind at breakneck speed: the piano, the clothes, the house in Atlanta, the kittens, the binoculars, the lilacs . . .

"You sent me the piano and the clothes!" she exclaimed. "You sent the telegram so you could get me up here, so you could get me into bed!"

"No! I mean yes."

How could she have been so gullible, so naive, so stupid? He *was* her fairy godmother.

"I wanted to get you up here, yes, but I didn't send the piano or the clothes. I didn't do what I did to hurt you, darling. The telegram was from Agnes. There *is* money, exactly as promised." He reached under the table and pulled out an expensive leather attaché case monogramed with the initials A.P.K. in gold letters. "It's all here. No checks you can tear up, just two hundred and fifty thousand dollars in cash. Enough to pay off your debts, enough to build your shelter."

She looked at him, unable to speak, staring at the gold initials on the case. He handed her the case, and she opened it slowly, eyeing the money that had meant so much to her only moments ago. Now it was meaningless. It was true! There were two hundred and fifty thousand-dollar bills inside. He was trying to buy her favors! He'd lied about everything!

"Where's Mrs. Finch?" she asked. "Can I call her?"

"She's out of town. Florida, I think."

"You're lying to me, Alec. This is *your* money, isn't it?"

"No, honest. Mrs. Finch—"

"Mrs. Finch, Agnes! And to think I believed you!" She wanted to cry, sob, scream. She waited for him to explain. She needed the money to save her farm and her animals, but she couldn't take money from him. Not for sleeping with him! She wiped her nose on the quilt. "I don't know what to do," she said to herself. "I don't know what to say."

"Say you'll live with me, Nora. Travel to exciting places with me. Be my mate, darling. Hire Mrs. Parnell and her husband to run the farm. Let them live in our house in Atlanta."

Live with him in Atlanta, be his mate, his traveling companion? Did he mean marriage? Things were happening too fast. She couldn't leave the farm, the place her parents had worked so hard to keep, the place where she'd planned for years to build her shelter. She loved him, yes, but he'd never mentioned love to her. Slow down, her better judgment screamed. Slow down and take one step at a time.

"What do you mean, *live* with you, Alec?"

"In my house in Atlanta, the one I took you to, darling. I'm only renting now, but I'll buy it if you want me to. You liked it, didn't you?"

"Very much, yes. But I thought the house belonged to Mrs. Finch."

"I'll explain about Agnes later, darling. Trust me now, if you can. Just say you'll live with me."

"Live with you," she said softly, unsure of the question. Still he'd made no mention of marriage. "What would your parents say?"

"They'd love it. They'd love you!" He took her hand. "We can move in tomorrow. Bring Wolf and Roy Bean, bring the flying squirrel, Dropoff, Mincemeat, and those ugly pups. I wouldn't want you without your animals."

She tried to remain calm, to speak slowly. "I'm confused, Alec. I'm trying to believe you, but it's difficult. I need money, yes, but I can't take money from you."

"But it's not my money, Nora. It's Mrs. Finch's!" He laughed. "I have money too. As much as you need. I never thought I'd be serious about a woman again, Nora, but it's happened. Don't ask me why or how. I just know I want you, Nora. You! I want you more than anything else!"

"More than the directorship of Markey's?"

"I thought I explained that."

"You did, but I still don't understand. I'm sorry, Alec.

I couldn't live with a man who does the work you do. A man who's against something as important as animal liberation. I'm sorry."

"You're saying my job with Markey's Primate Center is why you won't say yes?"

"That and other things. I guess I'm silly, but I believed your story about Mrs. Finch being my fairy godmother. I believed she really wanted to help me." She felt sick and got up to search for her clothes, going into the bedroom and locking the door behind her.

"Mrs. Finch *is* your fairy godmother, Nora. That money's from her, not me! She sent you the piano and the clothes. The house in Atlanta is hers too; I'm only renting it. Agnes is my housekeeper!"

"Don't lie anymore!" she yelled as loud as she could. She took the kittens into the bathroom and freed them to use their litter box. There was silence on the other side of the door. Then she heard Alec talking to Wolf, but she couldn't make out what he was saying because she was crying.

In a while the snow melted. They drove to Cartersville on cleared roads, leaving the mountain cabin behind them. The loving and touching and ecstasy were over now. Alec tried to talk, but Nora wouldn't listen, refusing his explanation, his hand, his caress. They reached the rest stop in record time, and Alec stepped out of Nora's van.

"I'll call you in a couple of days," he said, standing beside her window, looking like he had the flu.

"There's no need."

"I'll call anyway," he insisted.

She couldn't look at him. His name was on the tip of her tongue, his face stamped in her memory for ever and ever, her love for him piercing her heart. Feeling sick, she drove off with tears streaming down her cheeks and stopped to lay her head on the wheel before entering the highway, afraid to look back for fear she would see him standing there and waving, afraid she wouldn't be able to leave him behind after all. Afraid of dying because she loved him so much.

* * *

Several days later, Nora was back at the farmhouse sitting on the couch in the living room and listening to Eve and Mrs. Parnell.

"You're sure you're okay, kid?" Eve asked.

"How about some lunch?" Mrs. Parnell suggested.

"No, thanks."

"Have you tried to get in touch with Mrs. Finch today?" Eve looked concerned.

"Today and yesterday and the day before," Nora said. "The woman doesn't know I'm alive."

She kept remembering Alec in the cabin, hearing him murmur he wanted her for his mate. Could he have meant marriage? No, he hadn't mentioned the word once! Not once, and he'd had the chance. Damned if she'd live with another man who didn't care enough to marry her. Didn't *love* her the way she loved him!

"You'll never guess what I found out about the hunk while you were gone," Eve said.

"I don't want to know," Nora answered. "But tell me anyway."

"He's rich." Eve smiled. "Stinking, filthy rich. His grandfather owned a dozen coal mines in Pennsylvania and West Virginia, and his mother comes from old money on the main line of Philadelphia."

"He's not a doctor?"

"Oh, he's a doctor all right. The Center for Disease Control says he's one of their best. I called them when I saw this piece in Sunday's *Atlanta Journal*." Eve showed Nora a clipping from the society page with a write-up about Markey's Primate Center. "That picture was taken in a mansion in Atlanta," Eve said.

Nora nodded. "I thought the house belonged to Mrs. Finch, but now I don't know who it belongs to."

"That's the other thing I have to tell you, kid. Mrs. Finch called while you were gone."

Nora looked up. "She did? I don't believe it!"

"Maybe you'd better call her back. She's been away in Florida."

Alec had said she was out of town, in Florida. He'd been telling the truth! "What else did she say?"

"She said she didn't send you the piano or the clothes."

"Then she isn't my fairy godmother, is she?"

"No, kid, she isn't. The poor soul doesn't have a dime. She's Mrs. Gustavius Finch of Atlanta, not Mrs. Octavius Finch, the one with all the money. Agnes Finch is penniless and living on Social Security."

Alec *had* been lying. Nora closed her eyes to hold back the tears.

"I guess the hunk's your fairy godmother, kid," Eve said. "I'm sorry."

Nora was sorry too. She'd been so blinded by love that she'd refused to see what was happening. Alec had made a fool of her and blamed Mrs. Finch. Why? Did he have so much money that he didn't care what he did with it? So much money he could send pianos to a woman he barely knew? And lure her up to that cabin just so she would go to bed with him. "Damn him!"

"Now what?" Eve asked.

"I'm going to call everyone I know who hates Markey's Primate Center and get them to picket the place. The newspaper says he'll be taking over as director next week. I'll be there when he does!"

That night Nora couldn't sleep; she couldn't stop thinking about Alec. His words echoed over and over in her head as she tried to figure out what he'd meant when he'd asked her to be his mate. If only he'd mentioned marriage. But he hadn't. If only he'd offered to give up his directorship of Markey's.

Why had she fallen so hard for him? Her heart ached, and she turned into her pillow to cry. She cried a lot lately, feeling sorry for herself and trying not to think about what might have been. But it was impossible. Alec was constantly on her mind. Wolf laid his head on her back, and Roy Bean purred like a dishwasher. At least she still had her animals.

The following morning gifts started to arrive: ten dozen

roses in white, red, yellow, pink, and salmon; fresh bouquets of lilacs, and a brand new van.

"A new van! You must be kidding!" Nora exclaimed, waking up to find Eve in her bedroom.

"Get up, kid. They brought it to my house first because they thought you were there. I told them you lived in Loganville and offered to show them where. Come on, it's parked in your driveway. It's beautiful!"

Nora got out of bed and slipped into her robe, going out onto the front porch to look at the new van—white, with a tan interior and NORA'S ARK lettered on the side, along with a beautiful painting of an ark and all kinds of animals sticking their heads out of windows.

"Take it back!" Nora told the delivery man.

"Not hardly, Miss Flynn," the man said. "The van's been paid for in full." He handed Eve an envelope marked Nora Flynn and drove off. Eve handed the envelope to Nora.

"I can't open it, Eve. If it's signed, 'your fairy godmother,' I'll scream."

Eve opened the envelope and read aloud: "'For Wolf and Roy and all your friends. From someone who cares very much.'"

"It's from Alec."

"I know," Eve said. "The man's in love with you."

"Then why doesn't he say so, dammit? Why all this beating around the bush?"

"Maybe he has his reasons."

"What reasons?"

"Well, you haven't been very nice to him, have you?"

"I would have married him if he'd asked me, Eve, but he didn't. He didn't offer to give up his new job either. He doesn't love me."

"Then why all the presents? Men don't send women ten-thousand dollar pianos and twenty-thousand dollar vans if they don't love them."

"I don't know. Maybe it's some tax write-off for millionaires. Maybe he's trying to make up for the research he's done on animals. I can't figure him out." About to cry, she went back into the house. Eve followed her into the bedroom and watched her throw herself down on the bed.

"This isn't like you, kid. You've always faced up to things before. The hunk's crazy about you. You're making yourself sick worrying about him. What about the farm? If you don't find a solution soon, I'm going to call Alec myself."

"No, Eve, you can't do that. I'd rather lose the place first."

The dogs barked and howled, and Mrs. Parnell called to say a car was coming up the drive. "Now what?" Nora asked.

"Probably some sultan with the deed to the Taj Mahal." Eve laughed. Nora held her breath, hoping it was Alec. It wasn't. A big car pulled into the driveway; a man wearing a Stetson and carrying a briefcase got out.

"Nora Flynn?"

Nora walked out onto the porch. "Yes, that's me."

"Carson Henry, ma'am," he said, handing up his card. "I have a wealthy client who's interested in buying your farm. I've been instructed to offer you a million dollars." Nora held tightly to the porch rail in an effort to keep from fainting.

"Come in, Mr. Henry," Eve said. They went inside, leaving the dogs and cats on the porch looking in through the screen door.

"My client is ready to give you the sum of one million dollars, Miss Flynn. Is your husband home?"

"Husband? No, I don't have a husband."

"Well, that sort of changes things. I'm sorry. I was told you were married."

"I'm not. What if I were? What does that have to do with your client buying my farm?"

"Nothing, really, except that my client deals only with married couples. It's something in his upbringing, I understand. Well, I'm sorry I wasted your time—"

"Wait," Nora said. "You're telling me you can't buy my farm unless I'm married?"

"I'm afraid that's right, Miss Flynn. I'm sorry, but like I said, that's the way my client operates. If you can produce a husband, we'll pay you one million dollars for your property. But I need two signatures on the bill of sale and proof of marriage."

"One million dollars?" Nora laughed. "You must be joking."

"Some people might think so, but no, ma'am, I'm not joking. My client wants this farm for personal reasons."

"Personal reasons?"

"Yes. I'm sorry, but I can't tell you any more. If you'd like to call me, you can reach me at the number on my card."

"Thanks," Nora said, showing Mr. Henry the front door. "I'll be in touch."

She watched him walk down the steps to the driveway and waved as he drove off. Could it be true? Had she just received an offer of one million dollars to sell her farm? She must be dreaming! She'd wake up in a second or two.

She watched Roy Bean stalk a black female cat she'd never seen before. "Go on," Nora told the cat. "I know you've got a new girl friend and want to run off with her. Just remember who feeds you." As Roy disappeared into the weeds, the realization hit her: Alec wanted to buy her farm! But why? And why the stipulation that she be married? He'd never mentioned marriage before. Maybe she was wrong. Maybe it wasn't Alec at all. Maybe it was Mrs. Finch. But why? She scratched her head and decided to talk to Eve. Eve would know what to do.

"How do we know this Henry's legit?" Eve asked when Nora returned to the house.

"We don't. All I have is his word and his card. Don't ask me why, but I think he's for real, Eve."

"You believed Mrs. Finch was for real too."

"This is different, Eve. The man has a client who's rich, who will pay one million dollars for my farm. But

I have to be married. Who do we know who has that kind of money?"

"The hunk and the real Mrs. Finch."

"Right!"

"So...?"

"So I think Alec's trying to buy my farm."

"You mean you won't sell it to him?"

"I can't. I'm not married, remember?"

"So marry him, quick!"

"I can't marry him, Eve. He's never asked me."

"Haven't you heard of women's lib? Ask him!"

"I couldn't. I mean I just couldn't. You know I couldn't."

"I know you're desperate, kid. The hunk wants you to move in with him, doesn't he?"

"Yes."

"Then ask him to marry you."

"I can't do that."

"Why? Because you don't want to be married to a man who's trying to make things better for the apes at Markey's? Because the man you're in love with is rich? Wise up, kid. I hate what Markey's is doing to monkeys as much as you do, but it's not going to stop overnight. Maybe Alec can help. Maybe he's right."

"How can anyone be right who sanctions the use of poor, defenseless animals for experiments? Oh, Eve, don't tell me you've turned against me too?"

"Not at all, kid. I'm just facing reality. If someone offered me a million for my house, and I needed a husband to pull it off, I'd marry Doug Dunning."

"No, you wouldn't."

"Okay, I wouldn't. But you were going to marry him once, although I'll never understand why."

Nora thought about Doug. Why *had* she considered marrying him? Was it because he'd been there when she needed him? Because he filled a void after her parents had died? He'd helped her over a difficult time, and she'd mistaken what she felt for love. She'd never loved Doug. She knew that now.

"I don't understand why either, Eve. But that's not important anymore. Help me figure out how to get married by next week."

Just then the telephone rang. Nora was afraid to answer it, afraid it was Alec. What would she say to him? How could she ask him to marry her?

Two rings . . .

What Eve had said made sense. Maybe Alec could help the apes at Markey's. She wrung her hands. What was she thinking of? She hated Markey's and what they did to monkeys. She couldn't be married to its director!

Three rings . . . four. Her heart raced as she tried to get up her nerve. One more ring and she'd answer it. Five rings!

"Hello?"

"Hello." It was Alec!

"Oh, hello," she said, all soft and gooey, wiping her eyes and trying to sound normal.

"I've missed you, Nora."

"I've missed you too."

"Then why don't we stop this nonsense and get together?"

"I've found a way to save my farm," she said, wanting to test him, see what he would say.

"I'm glad, Nora." That surprised her.

"Yes, it's hard to believe, isn't it?"

"What?"

"That someone would pay one million dollars for my farm. The only catch is that I have to be married. Funny, huh?"

"Not so funny," he said, sounding sad. "I take it you're rejecting the offer?"

"I guess I am," she said, giving him a chance to say something. When he didn't, she asked: "Tell me the truth, Alec. Did you send me that piano?"

"No, Nora, I didn't."

She couldn't believe he was still lying to her. "Not the underclothes either, I suppose?"

"No. Mrs. Finch sent them. She's your fairy godmother. Please believe me, Nora. Agnes sent you those gifts, not me. Agnes gave you the money."

It was no use, he wasn't going to tell her the truth. She couldn't ask him to marry her. She couldn't live with a man who was deceiving her the way Doug had. Not even for one million dollars!

Chapter 11

SEVERAL DAYS LATER Nora took her place in the picket line in front of Markey's Primate Center. But her heart wasn't in her cause today. She hadn't been able to sleep or eat for days. She couldn't get Alec off her mind. He and his offer of one million dollars for her farm! Suppose he hadn't made the offer after all? Suppose someone she didn't know actually did want to buy her farm? It didn't make sense. Nothing made sense anymore.

"You don't look too good, kid," Eve said, helping Nora hold a big sign that said: ANIMAL RESEARCH IS ... SCIENTIFIC FRAUD! "Put your sign down and tell me the latest." Eve took Nora's hand and pulled her along to the parking lot. Twila held onto her other hand.

"I'm so confused, Eve. I hardly know what's what anymore. I think Alec's my fairy godmother, then I decide he's not. I think he made the offer of one million dollars, but I'm not sure. I honestly don't know!" Her voice broke, and she felt terrible.

"You're going through a rough time," Eve said. "What

you need is a vacation away from animals. Why don't you go off somewhere? I've still got my condo in Florida, and you're welcome to use it anytime."

"Thanks, Eve, but I can't go anywhere now." She got in Eve's big car and lay her head back on the seat, seeing Alec in her mind's eye, hearing his voice, seeing the color of his eyes, going over what he had said in the cabin and later over the phone. She was tired, she admitted; sleep didn't come easily anymore. Nothing would come easily from now on. She'd lose her farm soon, then she'd have to face giving the animals away. She remembered Mrs. Finch's words about finding a kind man and hanging on, never letting go. What a fool she'd been not to heed those words. What a silly fool.

"Are you asleep, my dear?"

Nora opened her eyes and blinked. Was she dreaming? Or had she heard . . . ?

"It's Mrs. Finch, my dear. How are you?"

Nora turned her head and saw Mrs. Finch looking in the car window, her bright gray eyes twinkling as they had that night at Symphony Hall. "How did you get here? Where have you been? I mean . . ."

"I came with a friend," Mrs. Finch said. "I heard you were picketing today, and I wanted to be here. I love animals too, my dear. All animals." She smiled. "You've got quite a turnout. There must be over two hundred people here."

Nora sat up in her seat, dying to ask Mrs. Finch some questions. "Won't you join me in the car?" She noticed Eve was gone. "I heard you were away, out of town. Is that right?" She opened the car door and Mrs. Finch got in, still wearing her voluminous pink raincoat, so long that it nearly touched the ground.

"Yes, that's right, my dear," Mrs. Finch said, closing the door. "Thanks to our wonderful friend, Dr. Knowles. He gave me a ticket for a Florida cruise, the dear boy. All expenses paid, of course. He's so generous." She smiled. "But, of course, you know that, don't you?"

"Yes," Nora said, thinking Alec was also untrustworthy.

"Did you like your piano, dear? It was very expensive."

"Too expensive, Mrs. Finch. I'm returning Alec's gift."

"Oh no, my dear. *I* sent the piano. Didn't Alec tell you?"

"Yes, but I thought he sent it. I mean . . . you mean . . ."

"Alec confided in me about your having to sell your own piano, my dear. He wanted to send you one, but he knew you'd never accept it. So I called my sister-in-law, Fanny—that's Gus's brother's wife, Mrs. Octavius Finch. I'm often mistaken for Fanny, but I don't mind. People treat you better when they think you have money. Where was I? Oh yes, Fanny was in Rome rescuing cats from some famous old ruins—I can't recall which one—when she heard about all the animals you'd saved. She wanted to help. Of course I knew she would. She told me to spend as much money as I pleased to help you and your animals, and to have fun doing it. So I did!" She smiled broadly.

Nora felt awful. "You sent me the clothes too?"

"Yes, weren't they lovely? I don't know what young women wear nowadays, so I had the buyer at the store choose them. I knew you and Alec were made for one another, and I wanted to help things along, so I invited you to dinner. You had to look smashing, didn't you? Forgive me for not being there, my dear, but you young folks didn't need me. Did you like the house?"

"It's beautiful," Nora said, anxious to find out the truth about the house as well. "How long have you lived there?"

"Only since Alec moved me out of my old place, my dear. He wanted to rent a large house, so I thought of the mansion Fanny's husband left her. She's never considered selling it before, but it just needed someone like Alec. Someone who could take care of it and bring it back to life. He's talked about buying it but says that's up to you, my dear. I do hope you two get over your differences soon. I rather enjoy being a housekeeper, especially for someone as kind as Dr. Knowles."

Nora felt as if she'd just run over a cat. She'd falsely accused Alec of being a liar.

"And the money, Agnes. The two hundred and fifty thousand dollars in cash. Did you send that to me too?"

"Of course, my dear. Wasn't that the sum you needed? Fairy godmothers can make mistakes. I'm not as sharp as I once was, you know. But I'd swear that was the figure Alec mentioned. Wasn't it enough?" Her eyes shone like stardust, and Nora threw her arms around her neck.

"I love you, fairy godmother!" she cried.

"Do you remember what I told you about my Gus?"

"I remember," Nora said, wiping her eyes.

"Then hang on tight, my dear. Alec loves you. Love is like the weather, you know. It has its storms and its calms, but when it's all over, there's always a rainbow. You're very fortunate, Nora. Love is a rare and precious gift which few of us ever experience." Tears came into Nora's eyes and she clasped the little old lady's hands, feeling better than she had in ages.

"I believe I'll go home now, my dear. I'm rather tired, and my friend will be picking me up soon." They got out of Eve's car and were walking through the parking lot when a big white Jaguar pulled up. Alec's car! Nora's heart pumped fresh blood into her veins as the tall, handsome doctor came toward them.

"Nora, I'm so glad I found you! I wasn't sure you'd be here." His eyes were warm and spilling over with something like sunshine. Nora squinted, feeling rosy and full of happiness. She held onto Mrs. Finch's arm.

"Alec, I thought you were gone."

"I couldn't leave without seeing you again, darling. Will you come for a ride with me?"

"I can't, Alec. I'm here to picket, and I've just begun. You can say what you want to say here."

He took Mrs. Finch's arm and helped her into his car, telling her he'd be back soon. "I have to talk to you, Nora."

"I have to talk to you too, Alec." She picked up her sign and fell in place behind a line of marchers who were all carrying big white signs decrying animal research.

"All right, I'll march with you. It won't matter since I don't work here anymore."

"But today was your first day as director."

His brows came together as he squinted down at her. "I gave up the directorship, Nora. I couldn't take a job that made you so unhappy. I haven't changed my mind about animal research, mind you. Not entirely anyway: But I've done a lot of thinking, and I understand your side even better now, the animal's side. As a scientist I'd like to promote reducing the number of animals used, employing alternative methods instead. We'll probably always disagree on the issue, darling, but Mrs. Finch made me realize our love is more important than anything else. I see that now."

Nora could hardly believe him. "Oh, Alec, I've been such a fool."

"No, darling, *I've* been the fool."

"But I didn't trust you. I thought you were trying to buy my favors. I thought *you* were my fairy godmother, when it was Mrs. Finch all along."

"You mean you finally believe me?"

"Yes, darling. Can you ever forgive me for doubting you?"

"I might, if you say yes to the following questions," he teased.

"I'm listening, Doctor."

"I bought a house yesterday. Quite a house it is too. Nicky and Myrtle like it. Do you suppose we could adopt them?"

"Adopt them?" she said, smiling up at him as marchers carrying banners and signs walked around them and stared, wondering what was going on.

"You're supposed to say yes!" He grinned. "You've

seen the house. It's huge; we've got plenty of property. Enough for a family and some pets. A few dogs and cats."

Eve stepped forward and handed Twila up to Alec. "She think's you're her daddy," Eve said. Twila, dressed in a blue and white sailor dress complete with hat, threw her arms around Alec's neck.

"Kids and monkeys like me," he said smugly. "I don't know why it is, but I like them too."

"So you want to raise apes?" Eve asked, walking with him and Nora.

"No," he said, "kids are more my style. Five or six, I think."

"Five or six!" Nora wailed.

He paused to look down at her. Eve detoured the marchers around them, explaining Nora was arranging for Twila's adoption. "You're supposed to say okay," Alec prompted.

"Okay. But five or six?"

"Not all at once, darling. You can take your time and have a few cats and dogs in between. I'd like to get started, that's all. Do you suppose we could go somewhere and lie down and talk about it?"

"This is where I came in," Eve said, pulling Twila back into her arms and joining the march. Alec continued to look down at Nora, waiting for her reply, his thick brows knitted anxiously. He was wearing a dark suit with a tan raincoat over it. The collar was turned up, just as it had been that night on Peachtree Street. Nora's hair blew in the cold damp wind and, shivering, she lifted his arms around her waist.

"Are you asking me to be your mate?" she inquired.

"More than that, Ms. Flynn. I need to know if you'd consider changing your name to Knowles."

She seemed to stop breathing as the marchers circled around them, and Alec held her closer, his eyes querying hers. "I love you, Nora," he said softly. "I guess I always have."

Her heart soared as the marchers chanted: "Stop animal research! Stop it now!"

"What about my crusade against Markey's?"

"That's your business. The Primate Center means nothing to me now. I've arranged to buy Twila from them. That's one of the reasons I came here today. I want to work with you, Nora. To build something good and lasting for us and for your animals."

"Oh, Alec, I love you!" She wrapped her arms around him and kissed him again and again, standing on tiptoe to reach his mouth. He kissed her back, lifting her high off the ground. The crowd of protesters roared with approval and threw down their signs and banners, clapping and hooting and hollering for more.

"Can we go home now?" Alec asked, oblivious to the applause.

Eve offered to take Mrs. Finch back to her house for the night. She waved to them as Alec helped Nora into his car.

"Where are we going?" Nora asked.

"You'll see," he answered, jumping in beside her.

They drove to Stone Mountain Park. Alec parked the car and took Nora's hand. "Come on," he said. "I have something to say to you up top."

She laughed and they ran up the path, climbing up the steep granite together, their hands entwined. The view of Atlanta from the top was magnificent. Alec stood in back of Nora and wrapped his arms beneath her breasts. As they looked down at the green earth below them, Nora sensed she was beginning a new life.

"Let's build a house on a mountaintop," Alec said. "We can design it together."

"But you already have a cabin in the mountains."

"Yes. It belongs to my father and me. We can go there anytime we like."

"Am I going to get to meet your parents?"

"Of course, darling. When I make you legally mine."

"Oh, Alec, I'm so happy." She turned and kissed him,

sliding her arms around his back and laying her head against his chest. She laughed out loud and ruffled his hair, slipping her fingers through its thick blackness, watching the wind copy her. "I like your hair like that," she said, pulling some down over his forehead. "It's the way you looked that first night on Peachtree Street."

"You didn't even look at me that night."

"I took a good look," she contradicted. "I said, Nora Flynn, now there's a hunk!" She giggled, and he pulled her back into his arms, shaking his head and smiling down at her. "Darling," she said, delighted because now she could call him endearing names. She touched his face, kissing him once, twice, all she wanted, holding him close and sliding her lips across his jaw, feeling the texture of his skin, smelling him, tasting him. He smelled good and clean, and he tasted wonderful, manly, and exciting.

"Do that again," he demanded.

"What?" she teased.

"Kiss me, hold me, touch me. I like it."

"Like this?" she asked, standing on tiptoe and kissing his mouth like a mother would kiss a child.

"Not like that." He frowned. "Like this." Holding her face in his hands, he bent down to caress her lips, circling them with his and opening them slowly.

"Alec," she moaned, breathless and excited. She wanted him to hold her forever, to never let her go, to become part of her.

"I asked you to marry me down there, Nora Flynn. You haven't given me your answer."

"Ask me again, up here." He looked deep into her soul, a sparkle lighting his eyes she wanted never to forget. She looked off into the distance, beyond his face and eyes, into banks of flat-bottomed clouds edged with silver. At that moment there couldn't have been a more perfect place for her on earth.

"Would you like to make a poor man very happy?"

he asked. His face was beautiful like the sky, striking like the mountain.

"Yes," she said, listening to the word echo on the wind. She closed her eyes and waited for his kiss. His lips mingled with hers in a kiss that made her rise like the clouds. She felt light and airy. Behind her closed lids she saw a million minute particles of love raining down on them, and rising again into the clouds, defracting the sunlight into tiny rainbows.

"I love you, Nora," Alec whispered. "I'll love you forever."

They drove to her farm and stood on the front porch for a while, just looking at each other.

"I think we should get married right away," she said.

"The sooner the better."

"This weekend? Eve won't have to work and we could be married in her pool house. It's such a gorgeous place, and it would mean something to me. What do you say, Alec?"

"Me too, darling." He nuzzled her ear, and she kissed his cheek. Lightning streaked across the sky. "There's a storm coming. We'd better go inside."

In the kitchen Wolf slid past them, and Smudge, the cat, raced between his legs to the bedroom where her kittens mewed. One of the furry babies crawled out of its cardboard box. Alec laughed and picked it up, holding it in the palm of his hand. "Looks exactly like Roy Bean," he said.

Nora watched him, thinking how kind and gentle he was. How could she have believed otherwise? How could she have thought he didn't care about animals?

Maybe in time Alec would join the defenders and elevate the rhetoric of the animal rights movement, conferring on it a respectability it needed. Now that she had money, she would work miracles, build the best shelter in the South: NORA'S ARK. She smiled, excited and happy, looking up at the man she loved.

"I have an offer to sell the farm, Alec. I've been offered one million dollars."

"Nora, darling," he said, still fondling the kitten, stroking its tiny ear.

"Yes, darling?" she said.

"About Mr. Henry's client..." His brows came together, and he frowned. "I'm the client."

"You?" she said in mock surprise.

"Yes, darling. I made the offer because you wouldn't accept any money from me, because I thought I'd lost you. I threw in the marriage stipulation in desperation to get you back. When you rejected me, I was heartsick. Then Mrs. Finch advised me to go after you, to hang on to you and never let go."

"Thank God for Mrs. Finch."

"Amen," he said, taking her hand and going with her into the living room. He opened the piano and played the hauntingly familiar "Claire de Lune."

Thunder rumbled, and Nora got a candle just in case the electricity went out. It was evening now, and she could hear the crickets singing. The storm drew closer but, sitting beside Alec and listening to him play for her, she wasn't afraid. The music was sweet and tender, like him. Few men could play with such feeling; few men could express such love. What bliss her life would be with him.

Nora heard a faint meowing on the sun deck and went to have a look. The wisteria were beautiful—lavender and white and fragrant in the night air. Thunder rumbled overhead, and she heard the meowing again.

"Lily?" she said, her heart light as she went to the edge of the deck and stared into the darkness.

"Meow!" came the reply, again and then again. "Meow, meow, meow!"

"It's Lily!" Nora cried, spotting her white cat at the base of the wisteria vine. Lily Langtree came running as Nora jumped off the deck.

"Is she all right?"

"She appears to be. She's skinny, but I don't see any

cuts on her." Nora picked up the cat she'd loved so much, and her happiness seemed complete. Tears streamed down her face. "She came home," she said.

Alec laughed and hugged her, her and the cat together, wrapping his arms around them and walking back into the house like a family. A real family.

Chapter 12

THE WEDDING WAS small and intimate. Nora wore an exquisite handmade white cotton dress from Mexico with a high neck, long fitted sleeves, and a forest green sash that trailed onto the lush lawn. Eve, the maid of honor, wore a lovely silk dress the color of Nora's sash, her blond hair cut short to show off her pretty face. Twila, the flower girl, wore a dress of misty green trimmed with Irish lace. When she threw several daisies from her basket, Eve said firmly, "Not yet, Twila! Leave the flowers in the basket till we get inside." The chimp squealed and ran to hide in Nora's skirt.

Mrs. Parnell met them outside the pool house with Lily Langtree and Roy Bean. The two cats were dressed in green velvet jackets and white bows. Wolf was there too, sporting a black velvet jacket and beret. Twila grabbed Roy's tail, and the cat meowed and hissed. "Behave yourself," Nora admonished.

The Wedding March began. Nora walked into the pool house, which was banked with spring flowers like the bouquet she carried—irises, lilies, lilacs, and tulips—and filled with golden sunlight. Twila followed Nora down the aisle, tossing daisies one at a time. People laughed softly at first, then more openly. Twila, frightened, let out a bloodcurdling scream, threw her basket in the air, and ran down the aisle on all fours to Nora. She leaped into Nora's arms, hooting and hollering. As Nora tried to calm her, Lily crawled up on her shoulder. Alec came forward from the other end of the pool house. Dressed in pewter gray with a white Indian shirt, its high collar open, he was smiling warmly. Nicky barked and came running too, followed by Myrtle, who wore green ruffles and old lace, a hot pink garter on her front leg and rhinestones in her ears. Nicky and Wolf met nose to nose as Alec reached Nora's side.

"Darling, can I help?" he asked.

"Take Twila," she whispered, handing the ape to him. Twila threw her arms around Alec's neck and screamed at the dogs, who were jumping up and down.

"We'd better get on with this," Alec said with a grin. "The minister's losing his patience."

"Okay." Nora smiled, filling her eyes with him. The music started over again, and they walked down the aisle with their family of animals to where the minister was waiting.

He cleared his throat. "May we begin?"

Alec nodded, taking Nora's hand in his and looking into her eyes. Nicky growled at Wolf, who fell down and rolled over, sticking his feet straight up in the air. "Nicky!" Alec scolded under his breath. Roy Bean meowed in his loudest voice and jumped onto a red cushioned chair beside the minister to see better. Everyone laughed, except the minister who was reading beautiful words of inspiration and heartrendering promise.

Nora looked up at the handsome man beside her. Nicky barked at Roy Bean, who took a swat at the dog's nose. Nicky bared his teeth and growled. Roy hissed and jumped down to hide behind the minister's legs. Clearly flustered, the minister stopped reading. His eyes bulged as Nicky dove for Roy and missed him by a whisker. The minister began again.

"Do you, Alec Prince Knowles—"

"I do!" Alec said.

"Me too," Nora echoed. Roy took off, with Nicky after him, Myrtle struggling to follow. Everyone laughed, and the minister pronounced them man and wife.

"You may kiss the bride."

"Do you mind holding my monkey?" Alec asked the minister, handing Twila over and taking Nora into his arms. "I love you, Mrs. Knowles," he said, his mouth on hers in a tender kiss.

"And I love you, Dr. Knowles," she answered fervently.

Alec took Nora's hand, and they ran to the car amid a shower of rice and flower petals. Myrtle got in the back seat of the car, followed by Nicky. Wolf barked.

"He wants to come too," Nora said.

"Do we have room?"

"Scoot over, Nicky," Nora ordered. Her eyes went to Lily and Roy in Mrs. Parnell's arms. "Alec...?"

"All right," he said, putting Roy and Lily in the back with the dogs.

"Bye!" everyone yelled as they drove toward Alec's mansion in Atlanta, the handles and bumpers of the car tied with white lilies and green streamers.

"I can see I'll rarely have you to myself, Mrs. Knowles," Alec said, glancing at the animals.

"Will you mind?"

"Not as long as I have you *all* to myself in bed."

"You will," she promised. "And I'll have you all to myself."

Just then she noticed a card on the dashboard that said: "Good luck! Your fairy godmother."

"She wasn't even there," Nora exclaimed. "I wonder if she really exists after all."

"Of course she does." Alec chuckled. "You still believe in little people and pots of gold at the end of rainbows, don't you?"

"More than ever." She sighed, snuggling close to him. "Especially rainbows."

COMING NEXT MONTH
IN THE
SECOND CHANCE AT LOVE SERIES

EYE OF THE BEHOLDER #262 by Kay Robbins
First he proposes, *then* he courts her...with picnics and
poetry, mischief and magic. Artist Tory Michaels is
totally undone by whimsical wife-hunter Devon York!

GENTLEMAN AT HEART #263 by Elissa Curry
For Alexis Celestine, convincing notorious ex-pitcher
Jake Shepard to make a beer commercial proves almost as
tough as fielding his incredibly sexy plays for her.

BY LOVE POSSESSED #264 by Linda Barlow
Like a man possessed, darkly powerful Francis O'Brien
stalks flamboyant Diana Adams across the Mexican
countryside, torn between his duty to protect her...and
his long-smoldering desire for revenge!

WILDFIRE #265 by Kelly Adams
Pressed intimately against the earth, with flames
leaping up all around, ranger Molly Carter struggles to tame
her wildfire passion for the sensitive yet
dangerously daring woodsman Sean Feyer.

PASSION'S DANCE #266 by Lauren Fox
Though she, too, is a veteran of a physically punishing career,
dancer Amelia Jorgenson swears she has nothing
in common with a "jock" like Randy Williams...
except, perhaps, desire...

VENETIAN SUNRISE #267 by Kate Nevins
Antiques dealer Rita Stewart steps into Venice and enters
a dream filled with vibrantly handsome, endearingly
roguish Frank Giordano. But is his glittering sensuality
blinding her to his darker side?

Second Chance at Love ®

___ 0-515-08204-X	FOR LOVE OR MONEY #230 Dana Daniels	$1.95
___ 0-515-08205-8	KISS ME ONCE AGAIN #231 Claudia Bishop	$1.95
___ 0-515-08206-6	HEARTS AT RISK #232 Liz Grady	$1.95
___ 0-515-08207-4	SEAFLAME #233 Sarah Crewe	$1.95
___ 0-515-08208-2	SWEET DECEPTION #234 Diana Mars	$1.95
___ 0-515-08209-0	IT HAD TO BE YOU #235 Claudia Bishop	$1.95
___ 0-515-08210-4	STARS IN HER EYES #236 Judith Yates	$1.95
___ 0-515-08211-2	THIS SIDE OF PARADISE #237 Cinda Richards	$1.95
___ 0-425-07765-9	KNIGHT OF PASSION #238 Linda Barlow	$1.95
___ 0-425-07766-7	MYSTERIOUS EAST #239 Frances Davies	$1.95
___ 0-425-07767-5	BED OF ROSES #240 Jean Fauré	$1.95
___ 0-425-07768-3	BRIDGE OF DREAMS #241 Helen Carter	$1.95
___ 0-425-07769-1	FIRE BIRD #242 Jean Barrett	$1.95
___ 0-425-07770-5	DEAR ADAM #243 Jasmine Craig	$1.95
___ 0-425-07771-3	NOTORIOUS #244 Karen Keast	$2.25
___ 0-425-07772-1	UNDER HIS SPELL #245 Lee Williams	$2.25
___ 0-425-07773-X	INTRUDER'S KISS #246 Carole Buck	$2.25
___ 0-425-07774-8	LADY BE GOOD #247 Elissa Curry	$2.25
___ 0-425-07775-6	A CLASH OF WILLS #248 Lauren Fox	$2.25
___ 0-425-07776-4	SWEPT AWAY #249 Jacqueline Topaz	$2.25
___ 0-425-07975-9	PAGAN HEART #250 Francine Rivers	$2.25
___ 0-425-07976-7	WORDS OF ENDEARMENT #251 Helen Carter	$2.25
___ 0-425-07977-5	BRIEF ENCOUNTER #252 Aimée Duvall	$2.25
___ 0-425-07978-3	FOREVER EDEN #253 Christa Merlin	$2.25
___ 0-425-07979-1	STARDUST MELODY #254 Mary Haskell	$2.25
___ 0-425-07980-5	HEAVEN TO KISS #255 Charlotte Hines	$2.25
___ 0-425-08014-5	AIN'T MISBEHAVING #256 Jeanne Grant	$2.25
___ 0-425-08015-3	PROMISE ME RAINBOWS #257 Joan Lancaster	$2.25
___ 0-425-08016-1	RITES OF PASSION #258 Jacqueline Topaz	$2.25
___ 0-425-08017-X	ONE IN A MILLION #259 Lee Williams	$2.25
___ 0-425-08018-8	HEART OF GOLD #260 Liz Grady	$2.25
___ 0-425-08019-6	AT LONG LAST LOVE #261 Carole Buck	$2.25

Prices may be slightly higher in Canada.

Available at your local bookstore or return this form to:

 SECOND CHANCE AT LOVE
Book Mailing Service
P.O. Box 690, Rockville Centre, NY 11571

Please send me the titles checked above. I enclose _____ Include 75¢ for postage and handling if one book is ordered; 25¢ per book for two or more not to exceed $1.75. California, Illinois, New York and Tennessee residents please add sales tax.

NAME_____

ADDRESS_____

CITY_____STATE/ZIP_____

(allow six weeks for delivery)   SK-41b

QUESTIONNAIRE

1. How do you rate _____
                              (please print TITLE)
       □ excellent   □ good
       □ very good   □ fair   □ poor

2. How likely are you to purchase another book
   in this series?
       □ definitely would purchase
       □ probably would purchase
       □ probably would not purchase
       □ definitely would not purchase

3. How likely are you to purchase another book by
   this author?
       □ definitely would purchase
       □ probably would purchase
       □ probably would not purchase
       □ definitely would not purchase

4. How does this book compare to books in other
   contemporary romance lines?
       □ much better
       □ better
       □ about the same
       □ not as good
       □ definitely not as good

5. Why did you buy this book? (Check as many as apply)
       □ I have read other
          SECOND CHANCE AT LOVE romances
       □ friend's recommendation
       □ bookseller's recommendation
       □ art on the front cover
       □ description of the plot on the back cover
       □ book review I read
       □ other _____
          _____
          _____

(Continued...)

6. Please list your three favorite contemporary romance lines.

_____
_____
_____

7. Please list your favorite authors of contemporary romance lines.

_____
_____
_____
_____
_____
_____

8. How many SECOND CHANCE AT LOVE romances have you read? _____

9. How many series romances like SECOND CHANCE AT LOVE do you <u>read</u> each month? _____

10. How many series romances like SECOND CHANCE AT LOVE do you <u>buy</u> each month? _____

11. Mind telling your age?
        ☐ under 18
        ☐ 18 to 30
        ☐ 31 to 45
        ☐ over 45

☐ Please check if you'd like to receive our <u>free</u> SECOND CHANCE AT LOVE Newsletter.

We hope you'll share your other ideas about romances with us on an additional sheet and attach it securely to this questionnaire.

• •

Fill in your name and address below:
Name _____
Street Address _____
City _____ State _____ Zip _____

Please return this questionnaire to:
   SECOND CHANCE AT LOVE
   The Berkley Publishing Group
   200 Madison Avenue, New York, New York 10016